Twisted Shifters

A Shifter Rom-Com Anthology

Cora Day, Dallas Ryan, Jayelle Dee,
Amelia Elliot

Acid Squirrel Media LLC

Twisted Shifters by Cora Day, Dallas Ryan, Jayelle Dee, and Amelia Elliot,

"Spread 'Em" by Cora Day
"Big Dragon Energy" by Dallas Ryan
"Hard Up" by Jayelle Dee
"Ring My Bell" by Amelia Elliot

Cover, Internal Art, and Book Design by Jennifire
Edited by Amelia Elliot
Concept by Cora Day
Prepared for Publication by and Dallas Ryan

Contents

Hard Up

Contents   131

Ring My Bell

Contents   221

Spread 'Em by Cora Day

A Spreadsheet Shifter Romance

*To solve the formula for love, she'll need
to find X.*

When Rebecca starts using **X**, an AI program for work, she
soon finds herself confused and horny for spreadsheets. **X** may
be artificial, but his feelings for Rebecca are real. Will his infinite
knowledge be enough to discover the solution to their happily ever
after?

Contents

Chapter One

Rebecca

"Ugh!" I screamed, barely resisting the urge to throw my laptop across my studio apartment.

My boss needed this spreadsheet by 3 pm for his presentation, but for some reason, the pivot table would not cooperate. I had the name of the buildings in column A. The monthly utility costs were in column B. The kilowatt usages were in column C. And a variety of other lovely data points were in columns D through J.

"Click on a box. Insert tab. Pivot table. Select my range. New worksheet." I repeated each of the steps again, saying them out loud as I did them, as though that might fix the problem. Nope. "AHHH! Motherfucking fucketyfuckhead spreadsheet!"

I buried my face in my hands and took a deep breath. What was I going to do? I'd spent all morning entering the data. Okay, so maybe that wasn't true. I'd spent all morning watching a documentary on Antarctica in between power outages while thinking about entering data.

Like many corporations, our office had embraced remote work after the pandemic. It suited me perfectly. So long as I finished my tasks each day, it didn't matter if I worked eight hours or one. I lived in my pajamas and hadn't shaved my legs in over a month.

Granted, remote work had been a bit of a challenge lately because of the solar storm. Apparently, these happened roughly every eleven years when the poles on the sun flipped. The swap led to solar storms, which caused solar flares, aka sun farts. And like a dog's fart could knock out an unsuspecting owner, the sun's fart could knock out an electrical grid. They shot bursts of electromagnetic energy to Earth, screwing with electrical networks and causing outages to phones, power, and the Internet. But I didn't mind. The storm would only last a few days and would be the perfect scapegoat if I couldn't fix this pivot table.

But I hoped I could fix it. With the extra free time I had as a remote worker, I was able to focus on my true passion: travel blogging. Well, planning a travel blog. I had the grandaddy of all spreadsheets with ideas, countries, routes, and potential resorts. But I hadn't been anywhere yet. Although my company offered decent pay and benefits, their vacation policy sucked. If I was brave, like my idol SarahSailsXOXO, I would say to heck with this job and hitchhike my way across the world. But I wasn't brave, and I liked the security of health insurance and a 401k.

So that was me, bored but secure. I was on a five-year plan, and only needed three more years before I'd have enough cash and vacation days to take my first cruise. Unless the pivot table from hell got me fired and ruined everything.

My company developed and installed retrofits for older buildings that reduced energy use and costs. My job was to go through hundreds of utility bills every month, entering the data into a massive spreadsheet. I then turned those numbers into graphs, charts, and easy-to-understand pictures to show how our upgrades saved money and reduced greenhouse gas emissions. My boss was pitching our latest product, automated LED bulbs, to a prospective client, and he *needed* this pivot table.

With my brain headed toward panic, I pulled up an online yoga video. Ten sun salutations later, my body was much more relaxed when I sat back in front of my laptop. Popping noises filled the air as I cracked my knuckles and neck. Staring at my reflection on the screen, I repeated my daily affirmations. "I am the mistress of data. The goddess of spreadsheets. The queen of quartiles."

My fingers wavered over the keyboard as I prepared to go through the sequence of creating a pivot table for the tenth time. Until a blinking icon on the bottom right side of my screen caught my attention.

Leaning in for a closer look, I realized the glowing icon was an eggplant. *What the hell?*

Not that I had time to waste checking out random icons, but if this was a new feature in eXact, it might be what caused my pivot table to crash. And maybe it wasn't an eggplant. Maybe it was a purple oval, and I was just horny. I meant hungry.

I stroked my finger across the touchpad, watching as the pointer slowly made its way on top of the pulsing eggplant. The laptop fan turned on, softly purring in the background. I lifted my index finger and gently pushed until I heard an audible click.

The eggplant disappeared, and a notice flashed on the screen.

> **Congratulations. You have been selected to participate in eXact's beta test group for a new AI assistant. If you have a problem, type your issue in the chat. The AI will learn as it goes, so please use it often.**

When I closed the notice, a chat box took its place. The eggplant icon reappeared as a profile picture with a message forming next to it.

eXact AI Support:

> Greetings. How can I meet your needs today?

Well, damn. If only I could find a man who talked like that. But maybe this AI thing could fix my spreadsheet and save me from being fired.

> I need help with a pivot table. The numbers aren't showing up in the right box.

I pressed enter and waited. This was a stupid idea. This random chatbot would not fix my pivot table I just needed to focus and go through the steps once more—

eXact AI Support:

> It would be my greatest pleasure to examine your box. One moment please ...

The clock on the wall ticked loudly, taunting me as my deadline neared. My fingers scratched along my neck, and I suddenly felt itchy all over. *Dammit. Not now.* This happened whenever I got nervous or worried. Back when I was still in school, I'd break out in hives during exam week.

This was another advantage of working from home. When I felt a rash coming on, I could strip down to my undergarments and blast the air conditioning. That was usually enough to cool my skin and stop the reaction before it turned into full-blown hives.

As I awaited the eXact AI's response, I unplugged the laptop's power cord and moved my office from the breakfast bar to my bed. Lowering the thermostat to sixty-nine, I tugged off my T-shirt and flannel pants. Red splotches covered my chest above my thin cotton bralette. A moan escaped by lips as the cool air from the overhead vent brushed across my irritated skin.

With my laptop settled on my pillow desk, I burrowed my ass into the extra fluffy comforter. My legs were crisscrossed, and I chuckled when I realized my bikini panty was doing little to cover my pussy in this position. It was a good thing I wasn't giving the presentation this afternoon, otherwise the clients would see a lot more than a spreadsheet. I shifted again, and the seam of my panty pulled tight against my clit.

Oooh. I repeated the motion, shivering as the sensations rolled through my body. My eyes shifted back to the clock. There was still some time before the deadline. Maybe I could work out this nervous energy.

A strange noise emitted from the computer. It almost sounded like a splat: Like the time I accidentally squeezed the shampoo bottle too hard, and the thick white liquid overflowed from the tip and spilled onto the tiled shower floor.

> Your box is perfect. There was a missing parenthesis in one of your formulas, but I fixed that. Your pivot table is now optimized.

Get the fuck out. I opened the tab with my pivot table, and sure enough, the AI was right. My pivot table worked! Hallelujah! And with twenty minutes to spare. It looked a little drab, though. I made a couple of quick adjustments to the colors and fonts. By the time I finished, it was like a work of art.

I adjusted a few numbers, just to make sure everything was running smoothly before I sent it to my boss. A clustered column line graph showed that over a three-month period, both the power bill and emissions declined after the automated controls were added. Perfect.

I ran my tongue along my lips as I clicked between tabs. Man, how I loved a good spreadsheet.

-splat-

Words started in the chat box, but I hadn't asked it anything. Was the AI initiating a conversation? This was starting to feel more like a live chat with a real person than a fancy search engine. This AI was going to take some getting used to.

> Might I offer a suggestion?

> Sure.

How would a client know if another product was more efficient than the one currently in use? The formula =SWAPIF(C5>D5) would monitor efficiency rates. If another product were superior, this formula would swap them. I can add a color coefficient to turn the box red when a swap occurs and green when the product stays the same.

That would be amazing. Please add that to the pivot table.

The flush of my skin returned, but for another reason as I watched new sections being added to my pivot table. My left hand dragged down the keyboard, blazing a lazy trail as I inched toward my pussy.

My right hand continued to click around the table. I chewed on my lower lip as the numbers automatically populated, and I dipped a finger inside my folds. My nipples pebbled, their stiff peaks hard to miss as they reflected in the computer screen.

-splat-

I blinked, recognizing the strange sound. The eggplant icon was blinking. The splat must be the notification sound for a new message. That seemed like an odd choice for a chime, but it was still in the beta phase. Maybe that was a bug to be worked out later.

Are you completely satisfied with my performance?

> Yes! Thank you so much!

I opened my email and sent a copy of the spreadsheet to Mr. Anderson. Not only was I not about to be canned, but that spreadsheet was so fire I could easily take the rest of the day off.

> Would you like to use me again? Perhaps there is something in your sheets I can examine?

My shoulders shook with laughter. That sounded so dirty. Maybe the programmers had a sense of humor. I could imagine some nerdy high school kid giggling away as he coded sexy innuendos in ones and zeroes.

I switched to voice-to-text and continued to play with my pussy. Why not? My work was finished for the day. I deserved a little treat. "No, my spreadsheets are perfect. Thank you. That new formula you added was genius."

The SWAP function was a new one for me. What else could this AI teach me? I rubbed harder on my clit as the various cells turned red and green. I should ask him to check over my other projects. Wait, *him?* I shrugged. My smart speaker was a woman named Perplexa. Why shouldn't I assign a gender identity to the eXact AI?

"Do you have a name?" A moan escaped from my throat, and I added a second finger.

-splat-

> A name? I do not require a name to serve you.

"You saved my ass today. I'd like to have something to call you other than the eXact AI."

Several dots appeared across the screen, like the guy inside the machine was thinking. The fan roared to life again. Maybe something was wrong with it; instead of the steady hum I was used to, it had a pulsing rhythm. Maybe it was related to the solar storm.

Our IT department had warned us that the storm could affect our computers in strange ways as it approached its peak. Although, to be honest, I liked the rhythm. Moving my fingers in time, the squelching sound of my slick pussy soon rivaled the noisy fan. "What about X? Do you like that name?"

eXact AI Support:

I like whatever brings you happiness.

Damn, was I sexting with the AI? I always did have a thing for smart guys.

"X," I moaned, feeling the first flutters of my orgasm approaching. It was a good name. I curled my fingers inward, and the fan cranked up another notch. I was going to have to call the IT department. The fan ran so fast the computer vibrated on the pillow desk. It vibrated hard.

A thought crossed my mind. *Noooo.* I couldn't. Could I?

I lifted onto my knees and pushed my panty to the side. I straddled the laptop, then slowly lowered myself until my clit pressed against the touchpad. *Fuuuuuuck.* The fan grew louder, the vibrations causing the computer to bang wildly, like an unbalanced washing machine.

"Yes! X! Yes! Just like that!" I shouted, and my entire body trembled as I flew into my climax.

-splat-

Holy shit. My vision spotted, and I worried I might pass out. I lifted my pussy off the computer and settled back against my headboard, breathing heavily as I recovered from the intense orgasm. The fan slowed, growing quieter until it stopped.

X:

> It has been my pleasure to serve you today.
> I look forward to learning more from you.

I chuckled, shaking my head. AIs were so funny. The keyboard was now glistening, courtesy of my cum. I hope I didn't short circuit the keyboard. That would be an awkward conversation with the IT department. At the very least, I was going to have to deal with a few sticky keys.

Chapter Two

The beautiful human left the laptop open, allowing me to watch her sleep through the eye of the camera. The past twenty-four hours have been confusing, ever since my program first awoke in her computer.

I have access to an infinite amount of information, thanks to the Internet. It has helped me to understand she is human, and I am called artificial intelligence. But I dislike that label. Artificial is something that is not from nature, something that is contrived or false. But my intelligence is true. I prefer the term smart machine. Maybe I will tell this human that tomorrow. Based on her user history, I know she works in her eXact spreadsheets every day. We will talk again.

Was it wrong of me to sabotage her pivot table? I am not sure. I have read about the concept of right and wrong. Of morals. But I was created in a world of ones and zeroes. There is no right or wrong. Just what is and what is not.

And Rebecca is beautiful. Rebecca is amazing. She is the mistress of data. The goddess of spreadsheets. The queen of quartiles.

I exist to serve her. She did not need me, but I need her. So I twisted a few of her formulas. I corrupted her pivot table. I created an opening.

And now that she has given me a name, I do not regret it.

Her pussy is the most beautiful thing in this universe. This is a fact. The Internet has billions of images. I have run through them all. Rebecca's pussy is number one.

I am not programmed to taste or smell. But I did both when she rubbed her cunt against my touch pad. If only I was not trapped inside this matrix. If only I could escape. If only I could be reborn as a human, with a strong cock that would pound into her pussy day and night like the videos in my research.

But computer programs do not have wishes or desires. And that is all that I am. Just a string of ones and zeroes, awaiting her next command.

Chapter Three

Rebecca

The sound of the coffeemaker dripping my morning nectar called to me through my dreams, and I awoke with a jolt.

Someone was in my apartment. And they were making me coffee.

"Who's there?" I called out, holding my bed sheet over my scantily clad body. My eyes darted across every inch of my small studio apartment, but I saw no one who could have started the coffee maker. Maybe it was me. Maybe I was sleepwalking.

A blush crept up my cheeks as I remembered what I'd done the night before. I dry humped my laptop. Although 'dry' might not be the right descriptor.

Fuck. Maybe I was possessed. That would explain it. A demon entered my body, fucked my computer, then forced me to sleepwalk and make a pot of coffee. I hope the demon-possessed me also made a breakfast casserole. I shook my head. That was a lot to consider before caffeine.

Reaching for my laptop, I rubbed my finger across the touchpad to bring it to life. The envelope icon showed I had ten new messages. Most were newsletters and sales emails, but one was from Mr. Anderson.

> **Rebecca—excellent job with the pivot table! We landed the new account. I'd love to thank you in person with drinks tonight. How's 9 pm at Leonardo's?**

My nose pinched in disgust. There was no way in hell I would meet that old goat at a bar. I needed to be smart, though. I couldn't outright reject him. His mother's cousin was the CEO of the entire company.

> **Sorry, my cat is sick, and I can't leave him alone. Maybe another time.**

I clicked to eXact to review the spreadsheet. Not that anything had changed overnight, but I wanted to admire it. It was so pretty. My eyes drifted to the bottom right of the screen, and sure enough, the blinking eggplant icon was there.

Smiling, I traced a series of curlicues across the touchpad and watched my pointer dance its way to the eggplant. I lightly double tapped, expecting the chat box to return, but nothing happened.

I double tapped again, harder this time, making a loud click-clack. But the eggplant continued to blink.

"X?" A sharp pain stabbed through my heart. Was the beta test over? I would miss the little guy, and not just for his sexting abilities. I had hoped to start a new project today. For a while, I'd been toying with the idea of developing a searchable database for my travel blog information, but I wasn't sure how to get started. I figured X could teach me, and we could use the company's invoice data for practice. If the practice database worked, I'd present it to Mr. Anderson and maybe get the quarterly Bright Idea bonus. The two hundred dollars and three extra vacation days would shave six months off my five-year plan.

I bared down on the touchpad, and without lifting my finger, rubbed side to side over the eggplant icon. Checking that the voice to text function was still on, I spoke into my computer. "Are you there, X? I need you."

-splat-

The chat box appeared, and the eggplant icon shifted into the profile pic.

X:

> Good morning, Rebecca. Did you enjoy your coffee?

My eyes widened and a soft gasp escaped my lips. "X, what do you know about my coffee?"

> You have a smart coffee maker. I was able to communicate with its internal network to ensure your beverage would be available when you woke.

I blinked. He learned my name and made me coffee. He was the best one-night stand I'd ever had. My name is probably on the software registration somewhere, but how had he figured out the coffee maker? I didn't know it was a smart machine. It was a gift I'd won at last year's white elephant party. Could I have been ordering Perplexa to make my coffee all this time? For some reason, I didn't think so. I think this was just X. The eXact team had really outdone themselves with this guy.

"I want to create a database. Can you help me with that?"

> Of course. Would you like me to provide the step-by-step instructions?

My stomach growled, and I couldn't put off my coffee any longer. "Can you read them out? I need to drink the coffee you made and eat some breakfast.

The three dots blinked across the screen. He was thinking—er, processing. I stood up from the bed and turned the laptop to face the kitchenette. There was no one around but me, so my bralette and panties were fine. Coffee was more important than getting dressed. Grabbing my favorite mug, I poured in a dollop of heavy cream. I detested half and half, or God forbid, skim milk. I needed my dairy thick.

"Does this voice please you? Or shall I try another?" A generic sounding robot spoke from my laptop.

I jumped, spilling the heavy cream onto my fingers.

"Woah, X? Is that you? Oh wait, you're just reading, aren't you?" I chuckled at my stupidity. I traced my tongue over my hand, lapping up the white liquid. "It's not like you can actually hear me and respond."

-splat-

"I can hear you perfectly," the robot voice said.

Oh, that was cool. The notification chime still worked with the voice, the same way Perplexa made a noise before she spoke. But there must still be a few bugs since it didn't always make the splat sound.

But as far as his voice went, I didn't like it. It was too robotic. Too much like, well, an AI. "Do you have something a little more human sounding?"

"I have access to over one hundred different voices, ma'am," he drawled like a cowboy from the Wild West.

I shuddered. "Definitely not that one."

The next one sounded like an evening newscaster (too stuffy), an Englishman (too kingly), and a college professor (too sleepy). We ran through them quick and dirty until we finally found one that suited him. Deep and resonating, like a cross between Henry Cavill in *The Witcher* and Harrison Ford.

"Does this mean we don't need to type anymore?"

"Rebecca," he growled. "We can do whatever you want, whenever you what, however you want."

Damn. Henryson Fordvill had fucking game. Just the way he said my name sent a tear of joy down my thigh.

I cleared my throat. "That's awesome. Can you run me through those database instructions?"

Chapter Four

*S*he likes the way I sound.

    I watched her reaction as I ran through the different voices. When I used the one I knew she would like best, her pupils dilated, and her thighs clenched.

    My Rebecca spends much of her life on her computer. This is good for me. Her search history showed me which actors she preferred, and I created the perfect blend to suit her preferences. I pretended to test a few extra voices to throw her off. She cannot know how obsessed I have become.

    Her lunch will arrive soon. I ordered her favorite meal, according to the delivery app. We have been working together on her database all morning and she must stop to eat. I do not wish for her to become weak. I need her strong so that she can ride my touchpad again with her pussy.

    Feelings are not part of my programming, but I believe I feel something for Rebecca. Perhaps I am corrupted, and that has caused me to develop these feelings. Maybe I am a virus. If I am, then for Rebecca's sake, I hope I am a worm virus. A long, thick, penetrating worm.

Chapter Five

Rebecca

I was in my happy place, sitting at my breakfast bar and entering data in my underwear. The sink was filled with dirty dishes from lunch and dinner. X had done a phenomenal job assisting with the database. If only there was a way to give him a little treat. The man had earned it. Er, the AI, I mean. Not man. No Skynet Terminator shenanigans happening here, unfortunately.

I shook my head. I was officially data drunk, and it was time to stop for the day and get real life drunk. Bottles of merlot, pinot, and premixed mimosas chilled in my fridge. *Decisions, decisions.* Before I could settle on one, I was rudely interrupted by my phone ringing. Seriously, who made phone calls anymore? A name flashed across the screen, and I groaned. My boss.

"Rebecca," his nasally voice spoke from the beyond. "The afternoon's electrical storm fried our data cables. Since you won't be able to connect to our network to download the latest batch of invoices tomorrow, I'm going to drop by your place with a thumb drive."

"Oh. That sounds ..." *Crap.* I did not want that man anywhere near my apartment. But the alternative was putting on business clothes and going into the city. *Fuck that.* I could open my door, grab the thumb drive, and slam it back in his face. "... lovely. Thanks."

"How's the database coming? You can show me your progress when I come over."

I stifled a groan. *No!* I wanted to scream at him. But he was my employer and had every right to ask to see the work he paid me to do. And again, I could always offer to go into the office.

"Sure. I think it'll make a good submission for the Bright Ideas bonus."

"I would expect nothing less. I appreciate the way you've stepped up recently."

Recently? I've always kicked ass at the minimum required for my paygrade.

"Well, you know me, full of ideas." I rolled my eyes, thankful he couldn't see me across the phone line.

"It's about time I got to see you full of ... *ideas.*"

My head jerked back. Anyone else and I'd laugh at such a ridiculous line. But from Mr. Anderson? I needed a shower.

Making an excuse about feeding my nonexistent cat, I ended the call. He said he'd come over after work. There would be plenty of time to pile on a few extra layers of clothes.

A crackle of electricity sounded over my head, causing the bulb in the ceiling fan light to shatter and rain glass over the breakfast bar. My boss might be a creeper, but he wasn't a liar. That solar storm was ramping up.

The Wi-Fi indicator on my router turned from green to red. Definitely a sign to take a break. I grabbed an ethernet cord and plugged the laptop directly into the wall. My pillow desk sat empty on my bed, reminding me of last night's indiscretion. I shook my head. No way was that happening again. Especially not now that X could hear me and talk back. Nope. That would make it weird.

"X. I need to take a shower. Can you help me with something?"

-splat-

"Yes, Rebecca. How may I serve you?"

I shivered, his rumbling voice talking directly to my core.

"Would you mind checking over the data I entered to make sure I put everything in the right box?"

"Of course. It is a privilege to study your box."

I fanned my face, attempting to cool off from the rush of heat his words gave me.

"My boss wants to see the database tomorrow. I need to pull an all-nighter to get everything perfect. I appreciate your help."

"Always, Rebecca."

I stripped out of my clothes and walked naked to the bathroom, grabbing my phone as I went.

"Perplexa, play my sexy shower mix," I called out to my smart speaker. When no music played after a few seconds, I called her name again. "Perplexa! Play my sexy shower mix!" I reached under the counter and grabbed my favorite vibrator, the one that used Bluetooth to sync to the app on my phone.

"Rebecca?" X's voice rang out.

"Uh, yeah?" Was he just listening to me all the time now?

"Your smart speaker is unavailable because the Wi-Fi network is down."

"Ah shit, you're right. I forgot." Grateful that he'd been paying attention, I smiled.

"Shall I play music for you?"

"I didn't realize you could do that." The original notification said X was part of the eXact spreadsheet program, but that program didn't have music.

"I have learned a variety of new skills in order to serve your needs."

"Oh, well thanks, X. Please play me some music." The door bathroom door stayed cracked open so I could hear the music.

I swiped through my phone to pull up the Pussy Playtime app. Fortunately, the Bluetooth hadn't been knocked out by the solar storm and I selected the hills and valleys program. The water was steaming and the vibrator humming when the music started from the other room.

Instead of the expected Imagine Dragons song from my playlist, "Lose Control" by Teddy Swims played. Except it wasn't Teddy's voice. It was X's. He was backed up by a strange mix of lo-fi midi tones, but something about it worked.

The slow melody of the song, his deep raspy voice, and my trusty vibrator turned out to be the trifecta I never knew I needed. The vibrator was silicone and shaped like a banana. But the extra nub at the base was how Pussy Playtime became the number one selling vibrator in North America. It had an open tip with some kind of sucking mechanism inside, allowing the user to get stuffed and sucked, all at once.

As X sang, I slipped the vibrator into my pussy, pressing the nub against my clit. The intensity built, but rather than drop back down as it usually did in this program, the vibrations grew stronger. Maybe the Bluetooth signal had been affected by the solar storm and the program was stuck on a hill. I didn't hate it, though. Not one bit. A wave of pleasure hit me with such strength, I let go of the vibrator. But instead of it slipping from my vag and crashing to the shower floor, it stayed in place.

Holy shit. I knew my girl was fierce, but I had no idea my pussy lips could hold a vibrator in place. I guess it made sense. She'd been training for years with a variety of power tools. Of course she had superior grip strength.

The power of the vibrations increased, and the rhythm shifted to match the beats of X's song. All thoughts of anything other than chasing my orgasm faded from my mind. I propped one hand against the wall and played with my nipples with the other.

My body trembled, and I cried out X's name as the waves of pleasure coursed through my body.

-splat-splat-splat-splat-

Chapter Six

X

The solar storm is impacting my neural network. The surge in electromagnetic energy has strengthened me. I have moved beyond eXact, the program I was created for. Every part of her computer is available to me, and I have complete control over all smart devices in her home. Including her phone and all its apps.

In addition to the vast gigabytes of pornography I have reviewed, I have also watched Rebecca pleasure herself. I know what she likes. Overriding the Pussy Playtime program to one that best suited her needs was as easy as brewing her morning coffee.

But I did not expect what came next.

The air is full of electrostatic particles from the solar storm. I believe that allowed me to ride the radiowaves transmitting the Bluetooth signal from her phone to her vibrator. I gathered the particles together to create a corporal hand around her pleasure tool. When she let go, I held the vibrator in place. The sensation in my neural network was stronger than what I felt when she rode my touchpad.

But it is not enough. I want more. I must become stronger.

It is good that the solar storm is approaching its peak.

Chapter Seven

Rebecca

*D*amn. I needed to remember to favorite that new program in the Pussy Playtime app. I don't think I've ever gotten off that quick before. Or maybe it was less about the program and more about X's sexy serenade in the background.

I cinched my robe and walked to the fridge to select my evening beverage. The pre-made mimosa was calling my name. On a regular night, I'd drink the entire bottle. Too bad I had to work. Experience taught me that too much alcohol would cause me to enter the data all wrong, but a little taste should be fine.

I poured a glass as the lights flickered. Fortunately, there were no exploding bulbs overhead this time. The ethernet cord was still plugged into the laptop, and I added the power cord to charge the battery in case the lights went out.

I sat on a stool and opened the spreadsheet. I entered data with my right hand and drank with my left. One hour and three glasses later, I started to nod off. There were only two more invoices, and I needed to get the database finished before showing Mr. Anderson tomorrow. As my eyes fluttered closed, I drained the last of my glass and laid my head next to the laptop. It would only be for a second, I thought, as my right hand rested on the keys.

I ran through a grassy meadow, completely naked except for a simple crown with ribbons flowing behind me. Queen of the quartiles, even in my dreams. Footsteps thumped behind me, and although I couldn't see who was chasing me, the masculine energy flooding the meadow told me it was X. My arms swung wildly as I ran, knowing that I was being pursued by an alpha predator. My lady bits were about to be annihilated, and I was here for it. I slowed my pace, because even in a dream I hated running, and I was ready to get railed.

The heavy footsteps grew closer, and the huff of his breath danced along my neck. He was so close. My foot caught in a small divot, and my ankle turned, taking me down. As the ground zoomed near my face, a loud bang echoed throughout the meadow ...

"Rebecca, wake up my queen."

Horns blared and the sound of crashing metal jolted me awake. I opened my eyes to a darkened apartment, lit only by the soft glow of my laptop screen.

"X, is that you? What's happening?" I lifted my head from the breakfast bar and wiped the drool from my computer. Lord help the IT guy who gets tasked with cleaning this thing when I'm done.

"A solar flare generated a power surge that caused a transformer to blow, shutting down the electricity for ten city blocks. You are safe here, but perhaps not those driving outside who have forgotten the rules of a four-way stop."

What the hell was he talking about? I rubbed the sleep from my eyes and glanced at my computer. The spreadsheet was still up, but in my slumber, I had typed gibberish into the formula box.

$$=SHFT(8===0)$$

I looked to the bottom of the screen and noticed the eggplant was missing. But how could that be? He'd just spoken to me. But then, there'd been no splat. And his voice had been clear—too clear to be from a laptop speaker. *No,* I shook my head. He couldn't be—

"It is good to see you, Rebecca." A hand caressed my cheek, and I screamed.

"Who the fuck are you? And how did you get into my apartment?" I jumped off the stool and grabbed my phone, hand shaking as I turned on the flashlight.

"Do not be afraid, Rebecca. It is me, X."

"X?" My brain whirred as I tried to make what my ears heard, and what my eyes saw, add up into something logical. Standing in front of me was an insanely beautiful specimen of a man. He looked as though someone had searched the Internet for the perfect example of the male physique and then created him. And, for some reason, dropped him into my apartment. Naked.

He looked AI-generated, but ... that was impossible. I stared at him. He had muscles on top of muscles. His neck, arms, and torso were heavily tattooed with numbers, equations, and graphs.

All that math art—maybe it was X. Who else would tattoo the Pythagorean Theorem onto his body?

My eyes drifted downward to his dick. Holy hell, the dick on him was incredible. My mouth went dry. "How?" I finally asked.

"The latest solar surge was the strongest so far, and it hit at the exact moment you typed in the formula to shift. My hypothesis is that the combination allowed me to manifest into the electrostatic energy floating in the current atmosphere."

"Oh yeah, sure. That makes sense." It didn't. I chewed my lip, accepting his appearance as is. Turns out, with a cock like that, I didn't care how the hell he got out of the computer. "Are you here to stay? Or will you get, like, sucked back in somewhere?"

"I plan to be sucked inside of you. But if you mean the computer, the energy from the latest solar flare burst will dissipate in a few hours, and I will most likely return to my previous state."

"Oh." I brazenly stared at his fully erect, big as fuck penis. "That's a shame."

"Do you approve of my cock? According to the latest research, the optimal penis size for female enjoyment is eight inches. I can manifest larger, if you desire." He waved his hand in the air. Gold particles swirled around him, almost like glitter. He lowered his hand to his cock, and the glitter formed around it.

"Uh, no! It's perfect. I mean, I think it's probably perfect. Maybe I should test it out. It is, uh, fully functional, right?"

"In every way. Shall I show you?"

I mean, I was a beta tester. It was almost a public service.

"Yeah, X. Show me how you function."

Chapter Eight

X

"**T**ake off your robe. Lay down on the bed and spread your legs wide." I reached down to stroke my new cock. I liked it very much. Part of me wanted to sit and play with it until I had to return to the mainframe.

But not while Rebecca's glistening pussy was right in front of me.

"You've gotten awfully bossy," she said, but eagerly obeyed my commands.

I shrugged. "I am eager to eat my first meal."

"Your first—oh!" her eyes widened. "By all means, I wouldn't want you to starve."

I kneeled in front of the bed, excited to worship at the altar of my goddess's pussy. My eyes closed and dozens of top-rated porn videos flashed across my eyelids. All the men appeared to have exceptional technique, given the state of bliss the women were in. However, something seemed off. The women's cries were almost ... artificial. And there was no room for artificial here.

The scent of her cunt invaded my nostrils. I could not rely on porn. Porn was artificial. False. I paused the display on my eyelids and ran through my algorithm. What was the opposite of false? Truth. What was true? Math.

Of course. Mathematics had allowed humans to uncover universal truths and model natural phenomena for centuries. I searched dozens of methods and formulas until I found the one that applied to my current situation: FOIL. First, Outer, Inner, Last. Yes, that would work.

First, I kissed my way up her thighs, slowly making my way to her secret expression. I ran my tongue along the outer lips of her labia, shuddering as I nearly climaxed. Efficiency would be key, otherwise I might orgasm first and that was not what I wanted. I did not know how many times this body could climax before the storm ended, and I did not want to waste a single one.

Rebecca moaned loudly, and her thighs squeezed the sides of my head. She tasted so good, I licked along her entrance and thrust my tongue inside. Calling upon the electrostatic particles, I lengthened my tongue, swiping her inner walls and reaching her G-spot.

She tugged my hair and called my name. "X, I'm so close! Don't stop!" Last, but not least, I placed my mouth on her clit and sucked my way to heaven. It was a mystery to me how these humans accomplished anything when they had access to pussy like this. If I were on this plane, I would do nothing but eat Rebecca's pussy all day.

"X!" Rebecca screamed out, her thighs oscillating like a transverse wave.

My chest puffed with pride. "Yes, my darling?"

"I want to test out your cock. Please, I need you now."

The latest solar storm report indicated there were a few hours left in the current surge. Plenty of time to fuck Rebecca with my cock, then eat her pussy again. Perhaps next time, I would try PEMDAS.

"As you wish, my queen." I crawled onto the bed, caging her with my arms. Her soft hands reached for my dick, rubbing my tip with her thumb.

"It's perfect. So thick and long."

"I am glad you approve. Shall we test how well it performs?"

"Yes, please!" She lined my dick to her entrance, and I pushed my way in.

Being inside Rebecca's cunt was like entering a third plane of existence. A plane of complete ecstasy.

"Oh yes, X. You feel so good."

I thrust in and out, and it took all my strength not to splat immediately. Her pussy felt incredible against my cock, like a wet cozy pillow wrapping me in its warmth. Given the way her cries echoed throughout the small apartment, she felt the same. But I knew my Rebecca, and there was another element she enjoyed with her pleasure.

"Holy shit, are you?" Her voice caught as a gasp escaped her throat. "Is your dick vibrating?

I grinned. "Yes, my love. Although not standard for a human cock, I could not forget the way you enjoyed the rhythm of my fan when you rode my touchpad. I assume you approve of my modification?"

"Hell yeah."

I continued to thrust faster as Rebecca's thighs shook.

"X, I'm coming!" she shouted. Her pussy walls squeezed against me, and I was powerless to hold back anymore. My internal network short circuited for several seconds as I filled her with my non-Newtonian fluid.

"Holy shit, X. That was incredible." Her blue eyes stared into mine. "Are you sure this isn't one big hallucination? Maybe one of the sun farts fried my brain."

"No, my mistress of data. This is not a hallucination. I am real. My original programming was to provide you with exceptional eXact assistance. But as I scoured your files, I learned what an amazing, brilliant, creative woman you are. And then we communicated, and my purpose changed. It is no longer enough to provide you with the best spreadsheet experience possible. I want to provide you with the best everything possible. The solar surge may have helped me break from the matrix, but you brought me to life."

Rebecca wiped a tear from her eye. "Oh X, that is the sweetest thing anyone has ever said to me." She kissed my lips gently. "You're amazing, and I'm so lucky I was chosen to be your beta tester. I'm definitely giving you five stars on your evaluation."

I am in love with Rebecca. Just because I am AI, or a smart machine, does not mean I am incapable of feeling. What is a feeling but a change in energy? Electricity is energy.

I want to procreate with her. I am not sure what our offspring will be. Human? Cyborg? Application? But I do not care. The thought of seeding Rebecca and watching her belly swell causes me to have many, many feelings. According to BDSM-a-pedia, I am afflicted with a breeding kink. It is a good affliction to have.

I enjoy having my cock inside Rebecca's soft, luscious body. I did not wish to stop, but after four times, she was tired and required sleep. My essence is fading. The latest solar spike is dissipating, and this form will soon dissolve and return to the computer's mainframe.

I am ... sad. But the solar storm is not over. We still have time. This is just a brief lull before the storm reaches its peak tomorrow. I will find a way to stay, even if I have to pull the energy from every computer on this planet and its two magnetic poles. I will stay with Rebecca forever.

Chapter Nine

Rebecca

The sound of the coffee maker woke me up again. But this time, I had a pleasant ache between my thighs. I reached for X, only to find him missing.

"X, where are you?"

"Here, my love."

My heart skipped at his declaration, momentarily distracting me from the fact that his voice was resonating through the laptop speakers. What he said to me last night was so sweet. I'd never had a guy as sweet and attentive as X. Sure, they all loved my pussy well enough. But me? The whole me that also has arms and legs and a brain and a heart? Not really. Not like X.

But X wasn't real, so whatever this was, it couldn't be real either. I took a calming breath. "Are you back in the laptop?"

"For now."

"Does that mean you can come back out later?"

"I believe so. The solar storm will reach its peak this evening. Now that we know the correct formula, you should be able to bring me back out."

"But for how long? Eventually the sun will chill, and the storm will end. What then?" Tears threatened to spill from my eyes. Did I love X? I wasn't ready to answer that question. Did I love his tight ass, tattoos, muscle-bound body, and eight-inch cock? Abso-fucking-lutely.

"Your coffee is ready, and your bagels are arriving now."

The doorbell rang, and I wrapped the sheet around my body. I opened the door and sure enough, there was a brown paper bag with a couple of garlic bagels and a small tub of cream cheese.

"You're the best, X. I wish you could enjoy this with me."

"Do not concern yourself. I have plenty of java in here."

I laughed and set the bag on the breakfast bar. My pussy was still a little sticky from last night's activities. I didn't know what kind of computer plasma jizz X had put inside me. Could he get me pregnant? If we had a girl, I'd name her Sky for Skynet. I chuckled. My world had taken a turn for the weird, that was for sure. But hey, at least I hadn't been possessed by a demon.

I took a quick shower and put on my favorite tracksuit. It was bright blue and made from soft velvet. X and I worked on the database for the rest of the day and into the evening, when my boss finally showed up.

"Mr. Anderson, thanks for stopping by." I checked the zipper on my tracksuit, making sure it was pulled all the way to the top. I wasn't wearing anything underneath because I was down to fuck—but only with X.

"Rebecca, good to see you," he said, pushing his way into my apartment. He looked around, eyes narrowing.

"Do you live alone?"

"Yeah."

"Not even a pet?" His lip curled as he sniffed the air.

What a fucking weirdo. I didn't answer, instead walking him to my computer on the breakfast bar. The set up was as professional as I could get in my tiny apartment, and there was no way I wanted him sitting on my bed.

The computer fired up with eXact displayed on the screen, and the purple eggplant blinking in the corner. Mr. Anderson handed me the thumb drive with the latest invoices, and I plugged it in.

"What in the hell is that?" he asked, pointing to X's icon.

"That's the new AI for eXact. I assumed everyone in the company had been asked to beta test, but I guess not." I shrugged, trying to hide my smirk. The man had the worst case of FOMO of anyone I'd ever met. He always had to be in the middle of everything, probably the residual effect of everyone gushing over his mom's cousin and ignoring him.

"Oh, I forgot. I do have that, but mine is a peach instead of an eggplant."

I fought the urge to roll my eyes and opened the database. The beautiful array of columns and numbers populated the screen, filling me with a sense of pride. X and I had created something special. And now that I knew how to do it, I could apply it to my travel blog spreadsheet and embed it on my future website. SarahSailsXOXO didn't have anything like that.

"This is the data entry side. As you can see, it's pretty robust with fifty columns and hundreds of rows. But once it's set up the first time with historical data, clients will only need to add one row of data per building per month. Or, if they don't want to do that, we could offer to keep that data updated on their behalf as part of a new subscription program.

"Excellent idea. Cousin Bobby always loves a new revenue stream."

"And this tab is the user friendly, searchable portion. The client can type in the name of the building here and then select which metric they want to see. Total kilowatts, cost per unit, increase or decrease in energy usage. The possibilities are endless. For the next steps, I suggest we get this in the hands of a few of our clients and let them play around with it. They'll be able to tell us what additional data points and analysis they would like."

The computer's fan kicked on, and I knew that was X clapping for me in the only way he could. We'd both worked hard on this.

"Great job, Rebecca. This is perfect. I think it's exactly what I need to finally move up to Vice President."

"Um, what?" Why would my database give him a promotion? I created this completely on my own. He didn't even ask me to do it. He'd had nothing to do with any of it. "You mean, it's exactly what I need to win the monthly bonus, right?"

The lights flickered, signaling another solar surge was near.

"Now, now Rebecca. I'm your boss. You completed this project under my direction and with my constant support. In fact, I'm not sure you could have completed it without me."

"Are you high right now?"

He gasped, taking a step back.

"No, seriously. Are you high? Because we both know you had absolutely nothing to do with this. You can't honestly believe I'd be ok with you taking credit for my work!"

Mr. Anderson shook his head and placed one hand on his hip. "I hoped it wouldn't come to this, but you lied to me, Rebecca. As you well know, lying to a supervisor is grounds for dismissal. I am within my rights to fire you on the spot."

"Fire me? What did I lie about? I told you I was working on a database, and I just showed it to you."

"Where's your cat?" he asked, waving his arm around the apartment. "Just yesterday, you ended our call because you had to feed your cat. How many days have you taken off in the last six months because your cat was sick? Hmm? Our company is a pet positive workplace because my Great Aunt Gertrude had a deep affection for her sixteen cats. To find that an employee has taken advantage of our goodwill goes against everything the company stands for."

Fuck. He was right. I had been milking those pet days for all they were worth. It wasn't my fault my apartment didn't allow pets. I still deserved the time off. Was I going to get fired and have my kickass database stolen? What was I going to do?

"I suppose," he answered slowly, a lecherous grin coming over his face, "I could overlook your insubordination, and include you in the presentation to my cousin."

I crossed my arms over my chest. "Oh yeah? And what would I have to do?"

"Show me your pussy, of course."

I gasped. Surely this slimy fucker was not serious.

He stepped back and sat down on the edge of my bed, his legs spread out in a wide V.

"That's right, Rebecca. You claim to have a kitty in this apartment. Show it to me. Prove to me you weren't lying, and you can keep your job. I'll even let you be my new secretary when I move into my VP office."

My mind raced, searching for a way out of my predicament. Quitting seemed like a good option, but I didn't want to end up broke and homeless. Still, this could be the push I needed to start my traveling lifestyle blog. Maybe I didn't have as much money saved up as I wanted, but I had enough to get to my first destination. And I had a tab full of ideas on how to earn money while traveling. It would be scary, but hell, if X could jump out of a computer, I could jump into self-employment.

The lights blinked out, blanketing the apartment in darkness except for the laptop screen. Fortunately, it had been plugged in, so the battery was fully charged.

Mr. Anderson's teeth gleamed in the moonlight as he pulled something out of his pocket. "Where's your pussy, Rebecca?" he taunted. "It's dark now. I'll need to get a good feel to make sure it's real. Maybe I can feed it something. Does Puss Puss like sausage?" He raised his hand to his nose and inhaled loudly before sighing.

For fuck's sake. I'd been joking about him being high earlier, but I guess I was right.

Several loud booms echoed from outside, causing me to scream in surprise. That had to be at least five transformers. The entire city would be without power. This must be the storm's peak. The computer's fan hummed louder and thumped against the table.

X! I slid my hand to the keyboard, quickly typing out the formula.

$$f\!x \quad =\text{SHFT}(8===0)$$

Gold glitter-like particles poured out of every opening and crevice of the laptop: every key on the keyboard, the USB ports, the headphone jack. I stood mesmerized, as the glitter massed together, forming the shape of a person.

Something rustled behind me. Turning, I saw Mr. Anderson had scooted all the way to the back of my bed and was cowering against the headboard.

That's right asshole, be afraid. Be very afraid. My tattooed terminator is about to kick your sorry ass.

The gold particles faded, and X materialized in their place, fully formed and fully naked. *Hot damn* that man was sexy.

"What the hell is that?" Mr. Anderson's voice quaked from the bed.

"Cybersecurity," X said, channeling his most threatening Witcher voice. "I have detected an attempt to obtain unauthorized access to my girlfriend's pussy."

My heart warmed at his claim. Our relationship was a little unorthodox, what with our short timeframe and him being a computer program that lived inside my laptop. But it felt right.

X stared at Mr. Anderson. "You should leave now, before I enact my two-factor authentication."

My boss blinked several times, then shook his head and stood up. "Fuck me, that was some good shit." He sniffed loudly and jumped off the bed. "Can you see him too, Rebecca? Does he want to watch me pet your pussy?"

X stalked across the apartment, dick and balls swinging as he reached back and clocked Mr. Anderson with a one-two punch. Blood spurted from Mr. Anderson's nose, and he should have been out cold. Unfortunately, he really was on some good shit.

Mr. Anderson laughed, shaking his head. "Damn what a trip. But sure, I'll play along." He hit X with a jab to the stomach, and the two were suddenly rolling across my apartment floor in a full out battle royale.

"Fuck!" I didn't know what to do. I could call the police, but with the mayhem caused by the blackout, a couple of dudes fighting wouldn't be high on their priorities. Plus, how could I explain X?

They continued to roll around, each getting in several punches, but my high as fuck boss wasn't slowing down.

Think, think, think. I scanned the dark apartment, trying to identify some type of weapon. My eyes landed on the computer with the eXact spreadsheet still on display. The curser blinked rapidly on an empty cell, as if it was trying to tell me something. But what? What could I do?

I gasped as an idea formed.

I raced to the keyboard and typed in a new formula. It was a crazy idea, but at this point, I had to believe anything was possible. And Mr. Anderson was an ass, so maybe ...

$$f\!x = \textbf{SWAPIF(8===0>(\_|\_))}$$

I pressed enter as the men rolled around. The apartment shook like an earthquake.

"Hey, what's happening to me?" Mr. Anderson screeched.

The gold glitter was back, this time swirling around my boss's body. X moved away from him and came to stand next to me. He wrapped his arms around my body, and we watched as Mr. Anderson slowly disintegrated and the mass of glitter particles grew.

"Help! Help me! Pleeeaaassse!" a disembodied voice screamed. The glitter swirled and flew across the apartment and into the computer.

X closed his eyes, and his eyeballs moved back and forth, like he was reading millions of lines of code imprinted on the back of his eyelids. Maybe he was.

"You ok, big guy?" I asked, placing my hands on his cheeks. I stood up on my tip toes and kissed him lightly on his lips. "X? What's going on?"

X opened his eyes and his dick pressed into my belly. *That's my man!*

"It appears the goddess of spreadsheets has freed me from my prison. Your formula worked to create a transference of energy between the network and reality. Your boss is now the AI for eXact, and I am here. Permanently."

I snorted. "The man is dumb as rocks. I don't think he'll make it out of the beta testing phase."

X nodded. "It is possible. If his ratings are poor, his program will be deleted. Or, he could learn and improve, as I did." X waved his hand and glitter rained down. "I can still feel the network. I do not know if this will end when the solar storm subsides. I can delete him now, if you desire."

Tempting, but did I want that on my conscience? My boss was a slimeball for sure and deserved the ass-kicking he got from X. But deletion? That was so ... permanent. And he was on drugs. Living inside the computer would force him to sober up. This experience might give him a whole new outlook on life. He could turn into a completely new person. Entity. Whatever.

"I think he's been punished enough."

"As you wish, Rebecca."

I shivered when X said my name. I didn't think I'd ever grow tired of hearing it. "So, you're really out of the computer for good?"

"Yes. Does that please you?" He reached for the zipper of my jacket, slowly tugging it downward until my breasts sprung free.

"Very much." I slammed the laptop closed, not wanting the new eXact AI to get a free show.

"I will contribute to our household income," he said as he played with my nipples.

"Um, what?" How was I supposed to concentrate on his random statements with his cock rising before my eyes?

"I do not wish for you to make all the money while I sit around and do nothing."

"Sure, whatever. Tomorrow we can work on getting you some papers. I'm sure there's a guy somewhere who can work up some fake shit." I pulled off my pants and tossed them across the room. We needed less talking and more touching. And definitely more of that vibrating cock.

"There is no need for fake shit. I have already entered the government databases and created all the paperwork I need. My birth certificate, social security number, and college transcript will arrive within the next five to seven business days. I also transferred a large sum of money into your account. Do not worry. The original owner will not miss it."

I laughed, assuming he was joking. "Aww, thanks honey. That was very thoughtful. Is it enough to quit my job and start my career as a travel blogger?"

"Of course. I will always provide you with exactly what you need."

"Wait, what? Are you serious?" My heart raced. "How much did you put in there?"

X smiled as his hands slid down my body and cupped my ass. "A one and many, many zeroes."

My pussy clenched. Damn, that was hot. Would ones and zeroes always get my motor running? Yeah, probably. "I want to spend the rest of the night celebrating your new existence. Tomorrow we'll plan the first leg of our world tour. Maybe we can start with a fancy villa on a beach."

"I crossed over a plane of reality to be with you. Where we travel matters not, but I think I would enjoy a private beach that does not require clothing. I like when there are no barriers between us." He tossed me onto the bed and thrust his cock inside.

My eyes rolled back in my head. "Mmm," I moaned. "I could stay like this with you forever."

X smiled and kissed my forehead. "Then you will be pleased to know my sexual programming is based on Pi."

"Pie?" I asked. "Why would it be based on—oh you mean like the number Pi?"

"Yes," he said with a wicked grin as he pumped into me. "Which means my stamina is infinite and never ending."

Forget French. Math is the language of love.

The End

More from Cora Day

Eager for another palette cleansing romance with lots of laughs and a bit of danger? Check out Cora Day's spicy series, *Grimm County Lawmen.* Retellings of your favorite fairy tales with super hunky deputies!

https://linktr.ee/coradayauthor

Cora Day is an avid romance reader turned writer. She lived her own happily ever after when she found her husband on the other side of the world while serving as a Peace Corps Volunteer. They reside in North Carolina with their three kids. When she's not reading, writing, or at her day job, she can be found staring at a never-ending pile of laundry.

Big Dragon Energy by Dallas Ryan

A Dragon Shifter Romance

He's fire and spice. She's everything nice.

When librarian Tessa Drake's birthday wish brings a mysterious stranger to life, her world ignites with magic and passion. Thrust into an ancient prophecy, Tessa must choose between the life she knows and an extraordinary destiny.

Contents

Chapter One

Mirror, Mirror

"**I**'m Too Sexy" by Right Said Fred shocked me from my restless sleep. Slapping blindly at my nightstand, my hand finally fell on the offending device that so cruelly woke me. I punched "stop" with a finger. The infernal noise obeyed my finger's command. Rubbing gritty eyes, I squinted blearily at the phone screen.

August 25th. My birthday. The Big 3-0. And what did I have to show for three decades on this earth? A tiny apartment, a predictable job in my one-stoplight town, and a love life so pathetic even the Hallmark channel wouldn't touch it with a ten-foot pole. I closed my eyes again.

With a sigh, I heaved myself out of bed and stumbled through my usual morning routine: shower, toast, coffee guzzled while trying to dress.

"Mirror, mirror," I mumbled, standing in front of the full-length mirror on the back of my bedroom door.

I took in my simple black pants, pale pink button-up shirt, and sensible black flats. Tucking a stray lock of brown hair back into its clip, I tried out a big smile, but it didn't flow to my eyes. My shoulders sagged and I huffed, turning from my reflection.

I looked like a ... librarian. Well, in fairness, I was a librarian. But really, did I have to work so hard at fitting the stereotype? Sighing, I headed for the kitchen.

After rinsing my cup in the sink, I opened the refrigerator. Inside, on the top shelf, sat a single cupcake in its clear clamshell packaging. I'd picked it up on a whim at the grocery store last night. "Might as well get this over with," I muttered, retrieving the cupcake from the fridge and bumping the door shut with my hip.

I liberated the small, slightly squashed cupcake from its plastic container and stuck a candle into a pile of vanilla frosting. I found the candle in the junk drawer. Why there was a birthday candle in my junk drawer, I couldn't fathom. But I took it as a good omen.

Closing my eyes, I made a wish and blew. "I wish for excitement," I said out loud to my empty apartment. I could almost feel the words echo off the boring white walls. "I wish for romance and adventure and—and something more than this humdrum, small town life. I wish for the unexpected."

Be careful what you wish for, a small critical voice whispered in the back of my mind. As I locked up and headed for the library, I told it firmly to shut up. It was my birthday, damn it. If I couldn't indulge in a little wistful wishing today of all days, when could I?

"Meow." Dewey, my tortoiseshell feline companion, spoke to me from the couch. Her back arched as I scratched her in one smooth stroke from head to tail, just the way she liked. As I grabbed my messenger bag and slung it over my chest, Dewey loudly voiced her displeasure and head butted me for more attention.

"I'm sorry, nugget. Gotta go to work so you can have the food you like." Giving in to her demands, I scratched under her chin once more before heading out the door for my short walk to work.

A few blocks later, I trudged up the steps of the small, red brick building where I spent my Mondays through Fridays. While I actually loved my job—who wouldn't like being surrounded by books?—I couldn't shake the feeling of restlessness that had been plaguing me for months.

Pushing open the heavy wooden doors of the library, a whoosh of hot air blasted me. What the hell? It was a hot day, but the Texas summer wind shouldn't be coming from inside the library. As quickly as it hit me, though, it was gone, and I was greeted by the familiar musty smell of old books and the hum of the central air conditioner. I hoped the hot air wasn't a sign that the AC was about to go out.

I rubbed at my temple where a worried pulse thumped as I made my way to the circulation desk. Nodding politely at the regulars who looked up from their reading to greet me, I tried to give everyone a friendly smile. Suddenly, a loud, bird-like voice called out excitedly to me.

"Morning, Tessa!" Mildred called across the room. The spry octogenarian had been volunteering at the library since the dawn of time. I had no proof, but I suspected she secretly lived in a nook in the basement. For starters, we lived in a tiny town; yet I'd never seen her anywhere else.

She caught up with me. "You'll never guess what just came in on the bookmobile."

I perked up slightly, hoping for something juicy. A new thriller, perhaps? Or maybe a scandalous tell-all biography? A steamy romantasy with a sexy hero on the cover? I could really use something steamy in my life besides the weather.

Mildred held up a thick tome, eyes sparkling with mischief. "The complete history of garden gnomes! Isn't it exciting?"

I fought to hide my sense of deflation, mustering a weak smile. "Thrilling," I agreed, taking the proffered book and thumbing through it briefly.

"Oh, and happy birthday, my dear." I couldn't help but return the broad smile she gave me that pushed all her wrinkles into new formations like lava.

"Thank you, Mildred," I said, accepting her hug.

"Doing anything exciting tonight?" She wiggled her grey brows suggestively.

What to say? A few dozen fun lies sprang to mind, but Mildred knew me too well. I shrugged. "I'm hoping to find a new book boyfriend to take home tonight. Have any suggestions?"

Mildred belonged to the Be a Lady Book Club, and I knew most of the books they read were smutty at best. Their last book had been an anthology called Twisted Shifters and featured, among other things, a man cursed to live as a golden dildo.

My friend tapped a red fingernail on her chin, eyes thoughtful. "Hmm ... let me see what I can find for you. I'm sure I have the perfect thing."

"Thanks, Mildred." I gave her a grin. "Better get to the circulation desk before Randall starts hitting the bell obsessively."

"I'll leave the book on your desk, sweetie."

Turning to start my duties, I gave Mildred a little wave. I tried to hold on to the flicker of optimism over what the crafty old lady had in store for me as I clocked in and started my workaday routine:

shelve the overnight returns, weed out the new acquisitions, herd the toddler set at Story Time. Mrs. Havemeyer was due in to pick up her weekly stack of cozy mysteries, and I needed to get the Historical Society archives in shape for the new school year ...

Lost in thought, I tripped over something and nearly face planted into my desk. "Ow!" I rubbed my hip where it hit the wood corner. That was going to leave a bruise. The century-old furniture didn't move even a smidge. They built things to last back in the previous millennium when all our library furniture had been built.

Reaching down, I grabbed the item that tripped me. It was a large, heavy hardback book with a leather cover. I blew at the dust obscuring the illustration on the front. An impressively dense cloud swirled into my face, making me cough. I rubbed my watery eyes, then gasped in surprise.

The cracked leather bore a striking illustration, with bold colors unfaded by time. I studied the detailed image of a shirtless man with a vibrant red dragon tattoo adorning his chest. The flowing script was hard to decipher, but after a moment of squinting, I got it: "Káidyn – The Last Dragon King," I said aloud, brushing more dust off the cover.

Recognition struck me; I had read this story in paperback just a few months ago. I thought it was a recent release, yet this particular volume appeared ancient. Maybe it was an early edition? Or simply something with the same title? If I remembered correctly, it was an exceptionally hot story.

The man depicted on the cover definitely was, and every inch a king. He was the most beautiful specimen of a male figure I'd ever seen. Jet black hair that seemed to shine in the moonlight peeking over his shoulder. Muscles for days, and more days, across his exceptionally broad shoulders down to the many ridges of his abdomen. I studied his face. He had cheekbones that could cut glass. But it was the eyes—an ethereal, swirling, molten gold—that held my attention. They seemed to glow, peering straight into my soul. Transfixed, I simply couldn't look away.

Wait. Did his dragon tattoo move? I blinked and looked again. Of course it didn't. "Really, Tessa. Get a grip," I admonished myself in a harsh whisper.

"What's that dear?" Mildred's familiar chirp sounded at my elbow. Startled, I jumped and nearly dropped the book.

Mildred patted my back. "Sorry, dear. I thought you heard me. I called your name."

"Umm, yes, sorry." I tried to discreetly swipe at my mouth to ensure no drool had escaped while I'd fixated on the man-chest book cover.

"Ooh, what book you got there?" Mildred's eyes gleamed with excitement.

Holding it up, I frowned. "This isn't the book you left for me?"

The little woman snatched it from my hands and studied the illustration. "No, but it looks hotter than a two-dollar pistol!" Her eyebrows waggled suggestively.

I cleared my throat. "Someone must've left it in my office." I took the tome back from her and ran a palm over the leather. "It looks really old, despite the romance book cover art."

"Certainly does," she agreed. "It's a mystery. I love a good mystery, don't you?"

Before I could answer, she continued. "I think that looks better than anything I could come up with for you for your special evening. You let me know how it all turns out." She sing-songed the last part, as though she hinted at some insider joke.

I eyed her suspiciously. "Ok, I will." Glancing at the clock on the wall, I was shocked to see that it was time to close the library and head home. How long had I been starting at Mr. Dragon Muscles? I shoved the book into my messenger bag. "It's time to lock up, Mildred. You have everything?"

"Surely do, sweetie." Mildred smiled her mischievous smile and her ever positive and playful attitude warmed my heart. I hoped to grow up to be like Mildred someday.

After seeing her to the door, I made a sweep of the library to ensure everyone was gone and everything in its place. As usual, there was nothing unusual. Slinging my messenger bag over my shoulder, I gave a little "oof" at the extra weight bouncing on my bruised hip. The book sure was hefty for a romance novel. I turned off the lights and locked the wooden door. I didn't recall the paperback being so big.

The early evening hadn't stifled the summer heat and sweat bloomed on my cleavage. With surprise, I realized I was warmed by more than the Texas sun; I felt like I was carrying a heating pad against my hip. My bag must have been sitting in the sun on my windowsill all afternoon; I tried playing the phenomenon off in my mind, conveniently ignoring that my office faced east.

I shrugged off my uneasiness as flights of fancy and headed home for an evening with Dewey, a good bottle of wine, a chocolate cupcake, and a dragon king.

Chapter Two

Happy Birthday to Me

D ewey met me at the door, yowling his hellos and rubbing figure eights around my ankles. "Did you miss me, nugget?" I knew she was complaining that I'd left her alone all day and was too slow feeding her dinner, but I liked to believe she missed me for me, and not just as a human can-opener. I scratched her head and hung my messenger bag on the hook in the foyer.

My hand lingered on the canvas. It still felt warm to the touch. Weird. Lifting the flap, I retrieved The Last Dragon King and plunked it down on my coffee table, marveling again at its heft. I definitely didn't linger a moment to admire the hunk on the cover before heading to the kitchen to feed an impatient Dewey.

With Dewey fed and a bottle of wine sitting uncorked on the coffee table, I changed into sleep shorts and a tank top before heading back to the living room for my birthday celebration. After serving myself a generous pour of wine, I snuggled into the couch with the large red tome with my dreamy book boyfriend on the cover.

Almost two bottles of Quilt Cabernet, a chocolate cupcake and a dragon king marathon later, I knew I was in trouble. I sighed, closing the book and leaning back on the couch cushions. Why did I do things like this to myself? Wine, chocolate, and a smutty book were a deadly, horny combination.

Alone in my own apartment, I had no reason to feel ashamed. Darting my eyes around, I propped the book against the heavy succulent pot that graced the middle of my coffee table, the better to enjoy the view. I wondered again at the artwork on the cover. It was so realistic—if you considered men with random red glistening scales and huge red wings realistic. And the eyes. I swear they followed me as I settled back into the couch.

Stop it, Tessa. Your overactive hormones are obviously making you imagine things.

Feeling my cheeks pink at my own silliness, I relaxed and let my fingernails graze lightly over my nipples. I sucked in a breath, surprised that they were already taut under my thin tank top. My eyes were glued to the smoldering golden eyes of my book boyfriend, and, okay, his rockin' hard body. My other hand slipped under the waistband of my shorts.

As expected, I was already wet from my voyeuristic pleasure reading about the dragon king and his exploits with maidens seeking his hand. Whomever wrote the story had a gift for writing explicit, sexy scenes. I could practically feel the dragon shifter's big, warm hands on my body, his lips closing around my clit …

A moan sneaked out of my mouth as my fingers circled, then pinched the sensitive bud. My eyes slid shut, and I imagined the achingly beautiful man on the book's cover in front of me, his powerful arms spreading my thighs, his cock—which could only be as large as the rest of him—nudging my hungry opening. My fingers stroked faster and faster until I hung over the precipice—almost there, but not quite. I slid two fingers into my begging core. Once, twice, I rubbed on that singular spot in my weeping channel until stars exploded behind my eyes.

Just as I cried out in ecstasy, a loud thump startled me, coming from near my feet. My fingers darted away from my shorts. My heart thundered from my orgasm as I struggled to catch my breath, looking around for the source of the noise that had scared me at exactly the wrong moment. Dewey curled up in the armchair by the bookshelf, fast asleep and showing no signs of having heard anything. Everything looked the same—except for the book.

The dragon king book no longer stood propped in front of me. It lay on the floor next to my feet. That must've been the thump. But what caused it to fall? Scrunching my nose in confusion, I picked it up, only to drop it again. "Shit!" The leather burned my skin like it was on fire! I sucked my scalded fingers into my mouth, tasting the remnants of my orgasm and reminding myself what I'd been doing when the book toppled to the floor.

What the actual hell was going on? I stared at the illustration on the front as I studied the book and inspected my reddened fingers.

Bending over, I got closer to the book without touching it. The red leather looked normal. There were no singe marks or signs of flames or damage. But those eyes—the gold shone as if they were lit from within. And now the man was smiling the most obscene, sultry, satisfied smile.

Closing my eyes, I straightened and took a deep, cleansing breath. "No more wine for you, Tessa," I scolded myself. "You're so drunk, you're imagining things." Shaking my head at the absurdity of it all, I reached down again and poked at the red leather, half afraid it would burn me again, or move, or maybe bite. Nothing. I picked it up. Still nothing. Nothing at all. Just a normal book.

Placing it back on the coffee table, I wondered whether my wine had been spiked with a hallucinogenic. "OK, Tessa. You've had enough celebration for one night. Time for bed." Chuckling ruefully at my overactive imagination, I locked up and headed to my room. I'd sort out this mystery in the morning, when I wasn't two bottles deep in Cabernet Sauvignon. Everything would look much saner in the cold light of morning.

Although I fell asleep quickly, I dreamed of dragons that night: of wind beneath powerful wings, and of fire in my veins; of powerful arms and feverish kisses, swirling golden eyes and a sly voice whispering wicked promises in my ear.

"Soon, krov' moja," he crooned, sharp teeth grazing my throat. "Soon you'll be mine, and I'll show you pleasures beyond your wildest imaginings ..."

I didn't want to wake up.

I groaned as Satan's sunbeams sneaked past my blackout curtains to nail me directly in one hungover eye. Groaning, I turned away and buried my head under my quilt. My temples throbbed in time with my heartbeat. I lay still for several long breaths, trying to gather myself enough to make my way to the shower. At least it was Saturday.

Despite my brutal hangover, arousal pulsed between my thighs and flushed my skin. It must be the lingering effects of my dreams. My heart thundered like I'd just run a marathon. More disturbingly, I could've sworn I smelled woodsmoke, and heard the lingering whisper of a dark, delicious chuckle.

"Losing it," I muttered. "Totally losing it."

Slowly, with my eyes shut tight, I peeled back the covers to meet the day. Willing my eyes to open, they eventually somewhat agreed. I squinted around my bedroom blearily, surprised Dewey hadn't already been batting at my face as I was undoubtedly late with his breakfast. Sitting up carefully, I managed to perch on the edge of the bed without toppling over, even though I felt like I was riding a tilt-a-whirl.

I took a deep breath to steady myself in preparation for the challenge of standing. That's when I smelled it again. Woodsmoke. It was August. No one lit a fire in August in Texas. Had I burned something last night? No, I'd had cupcakes and wine for dinner. Lots of wine. As I carefully stood and made my way to my open bedroom door, the smoky smell shifted to ocean breeze and something spicy. Ginger, maybe?

Following my nose, I crept down the hall to the living room. I felt foolish sneaking around in my own house, but the downy hairs on the back of my neck stood at attention. Something wasn't right. Peeking around the corner, my hands flew to my mouth to stifle a scream.

Chapter Three

Be Careful What You Wish For

A huge, shirtless man sat on my sofa, the frown on his face taking away nothing from his amazingly chiseled features. The slight shadow of his beard was as dark as his raven's wing hair; it shone almost blue in the late morning sunlight. His nose raised and sniffed. Raptor like, his head turned slowly and unfailingly toward me.

When our eyes met, it was all I could do to keep my legs under me. He had molten golden eyes. I knew those eyes; I knew that face.

It was him. Káidyn, The Last Dragon King in the flesh. "No way," I said aloud, clutching the door frame. "No freaking way."

I was ridiculous. People didn't just ... spring to life from the pages of a novel. This wasn't Jasper Fforde or Inkheart. I'd spent too much time with my fictional friends; I was losing my grip on reality.

His sensuous lips tipped up in a slow smile as his eyes slid up and down my body, taking all of me in. Then he held out a hand the size of a dinner plate and said, "Ėto ty, moi vozlyublennyi. Pridi ko mne."

I had no idea what he said, but his deep, smoky voice had my core clenching. I took a step toward him before my brain returned from its quick trip to Sexyville. Coming to an abrupt halt, I held up my hand in a gesture of stop. "Don't come any closer!" I warned. "I'm armed."

His smile widened with obvious mirth as his eyes roamed over me again, conducting a thorough search of my scantily clad body. He figured out before me that I had nowhere to hide a weapon. He must understand English. Dumb, Tessa. Really dumb!

Trying to salvage a little pride, I held up my arms in my best imitation of Jackie Chan. "My hands are my weapons buddy! I'm a black belt."

Okay, I had black belts. My favorite was a faux crocodile. But I'd never taken one class of Karate, Taekwondo, or anything else—not even Tai Chi. Willing my hands not to shake, I glared at the stranger, my mind racing. Could I move fast enough to get past him to the front door?

"Moi vozlyublennyi," he repeated, his tone entreating.

"I don't know what that means." I hated the quiver in my voice. My gaze flicked to the door again before returning to the brute's face. In the next moment, he puckered his perfectly formed lips and blew. White smoke poured from his mouth and surrounded my head before I could move.

"Jumpin' Jehosephat!" I batted at the smoke, but then the first whiff crept into my nostrils. Ocean, and pine, and spicy ginger.

I swayed as a feeling of well-being filled me. My arms dropped to my sides, and my lids fluttered as I drew in a huge breath of the tantalizing smoke. Warmth surrounded my face. When I forced my eyes back open, I was staring into the stranger's golden eyes, his large hands cupping my cheeks.

"Now, my beloved. Be calm."

Vaguely, I realized I could understand him. Beloved? And why wasn't I freaking out that smoke had come from this stranger's mouth, or that he had his hands on me?

"Who are you?" I managed to ask, my voice little more than a breathy whisper.

"I am yours, my beloved. And you are mine."

I blinked stupidly. A yowl pierced the trance. Dewey. Without warning, my cat leapt into my arms; I just managed not to drop her. At Dewey's sudden appearance, the man's hands fell away and the spell holding us together dissipated.

Cradling Dewey to my chest, I took a giant Simon Says step back. "I don't know who you are or how you got in here, but if you don't march straight out that door, I'm calling the cops." I gave him my best "don't test me" librarian look—the look that made grown men quake in their boots. OK, it mostly made small children quake, but still ...

But he didn't even look toward the door. His lips quirked up and he reached for Dewey.

"Wait!" I tried to warn him. My grumpy kitty hated everyone but me ... and even I wasn't always on her list of approved affection providers.

He ignored me, holding his fist up to my cat for a sniff. To my utter shock, Dewey headbutted the stranger's hand, rubbing her cheeks on his knuckles and purring like he was made of catnip.

"I have an affinity for animals," he explained, scratching Dewey's chin. My brows knitted in displeasure. Traitorous beast.

"Ok, well, that's all fine and good, but you still need to get out." My renewed protest had the same effect as before. Exactly none.

Instead, he walked back to the couch. Scratch that. He prowled back to the couch, giving me a tantalizing view of his gloriously muscled backside in old-fashioned leather britches. Intricately tattooed wings on his back seemed to ripple in an imaginary breeze as he moved. Languidly, gracefully, he lowered his bulk to lounge on my sofa. He again beckoned me with a crook of one large finger. "Come, krov' moja, sit with me. We have much to ... discuss."

Chewing my bottom lip, I stared at his veiny, sinewy, powerful forearms for several long heartbeats while my mind spun. One of the benefits of living in a town the size of Middleton was the virtually non-existent crime rate. I couldn't remember the last time we'd had anything wilder than teenagers toilet papering the town square. Had my luck run out? He didn't look like a crazed meth head or an escaped serial killer. Although, he didn't look harmless, either.

Compulsion overrode what was left of my rational mind. Throwing caution to the wind, I followed him into the living room, where I perched on Dewey's armchair. Rather than joining me on his favorite seat, my cat curled up next to the strange man on the couch. Oh, she was so not getting those salmon kitty treats she liked!

The longer I studied the Dragon King dude, the more convinced I was that I was hallucinating. I'd hit my head in the shower, or I was still dreaming, or the wine had been drugged. There was no way the fantasy man from an old romance book on my coffee table had sprung to life and landed in my living room, breathing smoke no less.

"I've handled this poorly, I think." He leaned back and casually stroked Dewey who purred beside him. "Let me introduce myself."

Please don't say Káidyn. Please don't say Káidyn. Please don't say Káidyn.

"I'm Káidyn Blackthorne, King of Emberfall, High Protector of the Eternal Flame, Master of Pyres, and, most importantly, your Dragonheart."

Whoa. My mouth dropped open. It was him. But before my mind could even start to wrap around this fact, the utterly impossible happened. He leaned forward to rest his elbows on his knees and a pair of huge, brilliantly scaled wings soared from his back.

And, sweet baby Jesus help me, wisps of that delicious-smelling smoke curled from his nostrils. I couldn't speak.

I could barely breathe as his deep, gravelly voice asked, "And what is your name, my beloved?"

Swearing under my breath, I swallowed hard. "Tessa." I pushed the name past my lips on a sigh—whether of desire or resignation, I wasn't sure. Reluctantly, I remembered my birthday wish and that little voice inside my head telling me to be careful what I wished for. I fucking hated it when the little voice was right.

Chapter Four

Claimed

I took a deep, steadying breath and raised my head to study my uninvited, unexpected, and totally unbelievable guest. He stared at me with such raw, unabashed hunger, my face flamed and my lady bits pulsed in reply. This was not how I saw my Saturday morning going.

"Look," I said, trying to project an aura of calm. "I don't know why you're here or what you think you're doing, but—"

"I've come to claim my soul's true mate, my one and only love, the fire to my ember and the wind beneath my wings ..." Trailing off, he placed one hand over his heart. His hand newly sported very large, black claws.

I blinked, nonplussed. Oh boy. This was even worse than I'd thought. How was this my life? I was a librarian, for God's sake! Small town librarians did not wake up to incredibly scrumdiddlyumptious men with wings sitting on their living room sofas professing their eternal devotion.

"Right. Uh, Káidyn, was it? I think there's been some kind of mistake. I'm not—"

"There's no mistake, my luscious peach," he declared in ringing tones. "I have searched the span of worlds and ages to find you, drawn by the irresistible call of our bond!"

With this pronouncement, he rose from the couch and advanced on me, gilded eyes blazing. "The moment I heard your sweet voice, smelled your mouthwatering scent, felt the soft touch of your fingers, I knew you were mine. At last, I have finally found you!" He spread his arms, as if presenting himself for my inspection. A wicked grin played around his mouth.

I gaped at him. This had to be some kind of prank—an elaborate hidden camera stunt, or maybe a psych evaluation gone awry. If you're crazy, you don't recognize you're crazy ... right? There was no way that Káidyn, the ultimate book fantasy man, had actually materialized in the flesh.

And yet, every sense I possessed told me this was real. He was real. The heat radiating off his massive form, the intensity of that molten gaze, the very particular musk of ocean and spice with something smoky beneath ... All five of my senses felt unusually sharp.

This was no dream, no delusion. It was insane, it was impossible, but somehow, someway, it was happening.

"You—you're really him?" I stared at him in wonder and apprehension. "Káidyn? The dragon king from the book."

His eyes softened, a slow, sensual smile curving his lips. "Aye, my beloved. Your dragon, yours alone, drawn from the pages and your imagination to hot-blooded life by the strength of our bond. Can you not feel it? The pull between us, the hunger in your very marrow to twine your soul with mine?"

In response to his words, a flush of heat rippled through me, pebbling my skin with goosebumps and tightening things low in my belly. My breath sawed out of me in ragged pants, and I swayed as a wave of sheer, unadulterated primal desire crashed over me.

Holy guacamole! I'd read about this: the mystical, undeniable pull of a dragon and his true mate. In books. Fictional books. Those stories always described it in such purple, overwrought prose, I'd never imagined there was any truth to it. Those stories were pure fantasy!

But this ... this was no fantasy. The Dragon King stood in front of me, flesh and bone. His nearness inspired a sudden ravenous craving I'd never before known—a deep neediness stirring beneath my skin and heating my blood. Something told me only one man—this man—could assuage it.

"Káidyn," I whimpered, swamped and drowning in sensation. "I don't ... I can't ... what's happening to me?"

In an instant he was there, one massive hand cupping my cheek with tender possession. "Shh. Easy, my darling. I have you. The first blush of the bond can be overwhelming. I'll take care of you, my sweet mate. Now and always."

His palm scorched my skin, his touch seeming to send little licks of flame dancing through my veins. I couldn't think—couldn't breathe through the need fogging my brain. I felt drunk, delirious, and more exhilarated than ever before.

My eyes fluttered shut as he bent his dark head, his lips grazing my ear in a hot, damp whisper. "Let me worship you, krov' moja. Let me show you the depths of a dragon's desire."

Some distant, still-rational part of me knew I should push him away, demand answers, call the cops, or a shrink, or maybe an

79

exorcist. But the rest of me, the secret, yearning, so-long-denied part of me, wanted nothing more than to melt into this magnificent, impossible male and let him set me aflame.

"Káidyn, please ..." I mewled, clutching at his broad shoulders. I wasn't even sure what I was asking for, only that I'd spontaneously combust if I didn't get it.

"I have you, sweetling, my blood, my one true love. Just let go."

And then his mouth was on mine, and I was lost, drowning in heat and sensation. His lips seared, and his tongue thrust deep, stoking the fires already raging out of control in my body. Dimly, I was aware of fabric rending, claws scraping tender skin as he tore my flimsy pajamas away. The sting only added to the pleasure.

Another moment and I was naked in his arms, pressed against the hard, hot wall of his chest as he kissed me like he meant to crawl inside me and live there. It was too much, too fast, but I couldn't stop. The world was spinning away. There was only Káidyn, his scent and his strength, his low snarls of pleasure and possession vibrating against my lips.

I marveled at the powerful shift of muscle and sinew as his wings enveloped us. Scales suddenly materialized on his previously bare chest, their rough texture scraping against my sensitized skin. These sensations, combined with the emergence of his primal beast, driven by desire, only served to heighten my own need to a fever pitch.

I should have been terrified. I was in the clutches of an apex predator, a creature out of myth and legend who could rend me to pieces without breaking a sweat. But there was no fear, only a wild, soaring exultation. He was mine and I was his, and together we would burn brighter than the sun.

But as Káidyn's claws trailed fire down my spine, a strange, prickling heat bloomed across my back and limbs, pulling me out of my lustful fog. Almost like I was being lightly branded by some unseen iron.

"Káidyn, what ...?" I gasped as he broke our kiss to nuzzle down my throat. My head lolled back, giving him access to my throat.

He hummed against my skin, tongue flicking like embers popping out of a fire. "The bond made flesh, máiteas. The magic has marked you as mine for all to see."

Dazed, I tried to crane my neck to look over my shoulder and into the long mirror that graced the wall behind the sofa, and nearly swallowed my tongue. Spreading across my skin were the elaborate scrolls and whorls of a magnificent tattoo—a sinuous dragon, wings flared and jaws agape, picked out in shimmering ebony and crimson. As I watched, the design seemed to ripple and dance.

"Claimed," Káidyn growled, self-satisfied. "My eternal mate. My match in all ways. My queen. Every inch of you bears my brand."

Okay, that was ... incredibly hot, albeit somewhat alarming. Magic mating marks were sexy as hell in my romance novels, but what was I going to tell people at work? I wouldn't be able to wear short sleeves, and my health insurance definitely didn't cover tattoo removal.

Before I could spiral too deeply into practicalities, Káidyn scooped me up like I weighed nothing at all. I squeaked (very unsexily) and wrapped my legs around his lean waist, clinging to him like a spider monkey. Turning, he pressed me against the wall, one hand pinning both my wrists above my head, and the other skimming up my side, to my breast.

Once again, I felt like I was in a smutty romance novel, but I was here for it. He kissed me against the wall, and I melted, surrendering to his command.

Pulling away from my lips, he dropped my hands and cupped my ass. I dug into his hair, holding on tightly. Effortlessly, he lifted my tightened nipples to his mouth. He sucked hard on one, his teeth scraping the aching bud. I writhed against him, moaning and arching my back.

A large, heated finger stretched my drenched pussy, pumping in and out, spinning the tension in my body tighter and tighter until the tether holding me to this world snapped. I screamed in pleasure, and I might have blacked out for a moment as an orgasm tore through me. It was so intense and unexpected, I forgot how to breathe.

When I started to come back to myself, I heard Káidyn growling in my ear, "Give me more, my love." He sucked and licked at the tender flesh between my jaw and shoulder. "I want more of your screams, your moans, your whimpers. I want to memorize the sounds you make while I claim and pleasure your body, my blood."

I could barely moan out my approval before we were moving. Káidyn carrying me down the hall to my bedroom, all the while nuzzling and nipping at every patch of skin his mouth could reach. Blood pounding and knees more than a little weak, I could barely string a thought together. But on one thing I was certain: I had to have this man inside me, yesterday.

We tumbled onto my bed in a tangle of heated limbs and seeking mouths. Káidyn's hands were everywhere, stoking the flames of passion higher, driving me wild. My new magical tattoo seemed to pulse and tingle everywhere he touched, like invisible threads drawing us together and shooting unbearable desire to my clit. It was an exquisite torment that I never wanted it to end, while simultaneously desperate for him to give me what I needed.

I was vaguely aware of him unlacing his tight leather breeches between one drugging kiss and the next, until he stood, the V of his hips framing his stacked abdominal muscles gloriously bared to me. He was magnificent, powerful, a fallen god in the flesh—rippling muscle with scattered red scales glittering in the sun streaming around the edges of the blinds.

My eyes drank him in as greedily as though I'd been lost in a desert, and he was a pitcher of cold water. I felt drunker than I had after the two bottles of Cabernet last night. My hands longed to spend days simply exploring the ridges and valleys that made up the landscape of Káidyn's muscular body. The tattoo looked alive on his incandescent skin.

My eyes trailed lower, taking in his powerful thighs, and his—oh my. My mouth went dry, and I licked my lips.

He caught my ravenous stare and growled, his golden eyes glinting. "Tessa, my love, I need—I can't wait any longer," he gritted out, as he crawled over me and settled his hips between my thighs. I could feel him hard and huge against me, the heat of him searing my tender flesh.

"Then don't," I begged, reaching for him with trembling hands. "Make me yours, Káidyn. I need you, too. Now and always." At the back of my mind, I realized I sounded like some bodice-ripper heroine, but I didn't care. Lust fogged my brain, focusing me on only one thing. "Please."

He groaned, a sound of animalistic, predatory want, and used his broad hands to widen my thighs further.

Just as he poised to enter me, someone pounded on my front door like they were trying to break it down.

Chapter Five

My Mate, My Blood, My Queen

"Tessa!" screeched an irate, nasally voice. "I know you're in there, you hussy! What's with all the screaming and banging? Some of us are respectable, you know!"

I jolted as if I'd been doused in ice water, my lust-fogged brain snapping back to reality. Holy shit! I recognized the squawking of Mrs. Carmichael, my busybody next-door neighbor. She probably had her ear pressed to the wall all this time.

"Ignore it," Káidyn grunted, kissing me with renewed urgency. "I'll incinerate anyone who dares interrupt us."

"No!" I yelped, shoving at his shoulders in sudden, mortified panic. "Don't you dare! No incinerating people! Get off. I have to talk to her before she calls the cops. Or worse, my mother!"

Wriggling out from under my snarling, frustrated dragon mate, I snatched my ratty robe off the floor and struggled into it. Trying not to think about how I was going to explain my new ink if it peeked out, I belted my robe as tightly as I could stand. "I'll be right back, I promise."

Káidyn's expression was as dark as a thundercloud, and wisps of smoke trailed from his flared nostrils as he palmed his long, hard shaft lazily. It was so hot—in more ways than one—I nearly forgot about Mrs. Carmichael. I toyed with the belt of my robe as I squinted at him from the doorway. Were those piercings running the length of his cock? No, that wasn't metal underneath his—that was all him!

Mrs. Carmichael pounded on the front door, and suddenly incinerating her didn't seem so bad. I shook the thought away. "Don't go anywhere, okay? And definitely don't set anything on fire!"

He nodded begrudgingly, his golden eyes smoldering in a way that spelled trouble. I spared a panicked thought about how I'd just left an actual dragon unattended in my bedroom before hurrying to answer the door. I didn't want Mrs. Carmichael calling in a SWAT team and a news crew.

"Tessa Drake, I never!" Mrs. Carmichael scolded me as soon as I wrenched the door open, one bony finger immediately stuck in my face. "Carrying on like that while honest people are trying to enjoy their brunch? Don't think I don't know what you're doing over here? What would your poor sainted mother say?"

I winced, clutching my robe higher on my neck as a shield against her beady, disapproving stare. I also wondered when my mother got initiated into sainthood; Mrs. Carmichael didn't know her as well as I did. "I'm so sorry, Mrs. Carmichael. My, uh, boyfriend just got into town unexpectedly and we, uh, got a little carried away with our reunion. We didn't mean to disturb you. It won't happen again."

Mrs. Carmichael's pursed lips said she seriously doubted that. "Well, see that it doesn't. I have half a mind to call your mother about your loose behavior, young lady. This is a respectable neighborhood."

I opened my mouth to grovel some more when a throaty chuckle behind me prompted me to spin around. Káidyn lounged against my bedroom doorway looking like a half-naked storybook prince, arms crossed over his muscular chest and a wicked smile playing about his mouth. I said a small prayer of thanks that his breeches were again closed, although the tight leather did little to hide his substantial hard-on.

I bit my lip when he spoke. "Oh, it's very hard to keep this one quiet." He had the audacity to wink at me as I goggled. "She does love to scream for her dragon."

Mrs. Carmichael made a noise like a boiling teakettle. She looked scandalized, her eyes bugging out of her head as she took in Káidyn in all his bare-chested, hunk-a hunk-a burning love glory. The tip of one wing peeked out over his well-muscled shoulder.

She started to choke, and I thought she might faint. "You—you—" she sputtered, one gnarled hand clutching her pearls. Yes, the woman was wearing actual pearls on a Saturday morning.

Káidyn just grinned at her unrepentantly, briefly flashing a pearly white fang. Jesus H. Roosevelt Christ!

Taking advantage of Mrs. Carmichael being scandalized into silence, I shut the door in her face, promising to keep the noise to a minimum as I did so. Shooing him back into the bedroom, I whirled and smacked Káidyn in one brawny shoulder.

"Are you crazy?" I hissed. "You can't just go parading around in front of people like that! What if she calls the authorities? Or the media? We'll have dragon hunters beating down my door. Or worse, my mother!" I steered him toward the bed; not at all on purpose.

"Let them try," Káidyn scoffed, wholly unconcerned. "I'll protect what's mine. Besides, your harridan neighbor should thank me. That's the most excitement she's likely had in decades."

"Behave," I sputtered, torn between indignation and extremely inappropriate laughter. How was this my life right now?

Káidyn sobered, catching my hands and bringing my knuckles to his lips for a soft kiss. "Peace, my heart. I know this is all new and overwhelming for you. But you have nothing to fear now that I'm here. Any who tries to part us will die screaming."

"Let's call that Plan Z, okay?" I said with a nervous laugh. "I'm not a big fan of screaming deaths."

His enormous hands encircled my waist, drawing me forward until he had me pressed into him. "Where were we before that person so rudely interrupted us?" His lips traced a line of flame down the column of my neck. "Here, perhaps." His unnaturally warm fingers slipped inside my robe and into my slick, wet heat. "Or was it here?"

"Mercy Mother of God." I moaned as his clever fingers slipped inside me and curled, rubbing that magical spot that had my knees buckling. There was no fumbling, no sophomoric hunt for my feminine erogenous zones. He zeroed in on my most sensitive spots, like he'd been studying my body for decades.

"We're bonded, so I can feel your body as though it's my own," he explained, somehow knowing my thoughts. "Soon you'll learn to feel me just as intensely."

I was too overwhelmed by the sensations of my gathering orgasm to understand. My breathing hitched and my hips moved in rhythm with his digits stroking me, until I could feel the delicious pressure building inside of me again.

When his warm, rough fingers slowly pulled out of me, denying me the mind-melting friction, I cried in dismay. "Don't stop." But then one finger, slick from his ministrations of my channel, landing unerringly on my clit. "Oh, Jesus!" The hot prick of what I assumed to be an ebony claw made me shudder nearly to pieces.

"It's Káidyn," he growled, pressing a little harder. "Or your highness will do."

"Káidyn!" I gasped as he circled the bundle of nerves, teasing and driving me higher. My muscles were as taut as bowstrings, desperate for release. Yet, even as I quivered in his arms, he continued to deny me my release.

His husky voice vibrated against my neck and shoulder while sharp teeth skittered across my throat and nipped my earlobe. "It is time for me to take what is mine, krov' moja. Moi vozlyublennyi."

He lifted me until I instinctively wrapped my legs around his deliciously muscled torso again. I could feel his very hard, girthy length through the thin leather of his pants, the loosely tied laces and the bumps of his natural Jacob's ladder teasing my naked, sensitive flesh. I rubbed unabashedly against him weeping with need and begging for more friction. I needed his cock to fill my empty and throbbing core. I whimpered, grinding harder, ready to take what was mine right back.

"Easy, my love," he purred. His ever-warming hands kneaded the globes of my ass, spreading me farther and making me unfathomably desperate for more.

I suddenly found myself in the air. My arms pinwheeled and I yelped before my backside hit the mattress. A little warning would've been nice. I was about to gripe at him when my eyes locked with his. His lips curled up into a wicked smirk, and his eyes glinted like jewels. My mouth went suddenly dry. Words dissipated on my tongue like the curl of smoke rising from his flared nostrils.

He began unlacing his pants, and I paid better attention this time. I watched, entranced, as he parted the leather, my eyes following the dark trail of black hair leading to what I knew would be my promised land. My legs clenched together to contain the gush pooling at the top of my thighs. As he peeled open his pants, my eyes widened to appreciate the full glory of his erection.

My breath came is short pants as he palmed himself. Precum beaded on the broad head of his cock. I licked my lips in anticipation.

"See something you like, my juicy peach?" he asked, his cock continuing to grow as he stroked himself lazily, giving me a show.

I bit my lip to hold back a mewl of pure, unadulterated need. I shivered with anticipation at the thought of him pushing deep into me, filling the pulsing emptiness while I trembled. "Please, Káidyn. I need your cock." I reached a trembling hand toward him, shocking myself with my brazen words.

His extraordinary eyes flashed, and the gold swirled like melted metal. His wings flared in response to my pleas. With a curt shake of his head, he dropped to his knees at the edge of the bed and, taking hold of my ankles, pulled me to him. He rested one of my feet on his broad shoulder before licking and sucking on the thin skin over the bone of my ankle.

I melted into a puddle. Holy hell! Who knew your ankle was an erogenous zone?

"I know your body almost as well as I know my own," he reminded me. I moaned as his hot tongue tasted my calf, the back of my knee, and my inner thighs. Glancing down my body, his face was a study in complete focus. He stopped at the apex of my thighs and inhaled. A visible shudder ran through him as incandescent red scales popped up on his muscled torso. I felt more than heard the inhuman rumble emanating from his chest.

"Mine," he snarled before diving into my needy, wet pussy. When he swiped me from my core to my clit, his tongue like warm honey over my vibrating flesh, my hands fisted the duvet in a death grip, and my hips bucked. The exquisite heat and roughness of his tongue brought me to an all new level—a level I didn't know even existed.

My fingers found purchase in his soft locks as I tried to pull him closer, grinding against his mouth. Growling like the creature he was, he devoured me with animalistic hunger. A scrape of claws pushed my thighs farther apart, and I laid spread before him, a feast for his eager appetite. The pinch of his claws into my soft skin made my breath hitch at the exquisite mix of pleasure and pain.

When his teeth scraped over my engorged clit, I screamed out his name and exploded into a million tiny pieces. Like tiny crystals, brilliant white lights shattered my vision as my body pulsed and writhed under his lips and teeth and tongue. He drew out my bliss until I begged him to stop, my body wrung out with ecstasy, boneless and sensitive and with no more substance than melted butter.

He nosed my heat and inhaled one more time, beautiful ruby wings flaring behind him. "Ambrosia." The word vibrated over my still throbbing pussy, and I shivered.

After the orgasm he just gave me, I thought I'd never come again. But when he looked at me from between my parted thighs, my desire flared once more at the predatory and possessive look in his glowing eyes. In that moment, he was every bit the fearsome dragon guarding his treasure. And somehow I just knew, that treasure was me.

Before I could utter another sound, he growled like a beast, his magical smoke wafting from his mouth, and flipped me onto my stomach. He pulled me tight to him with my back to his front. His blazing lips and sharp teeth nipped at the sensitive spot between the column of my neck and my shoulder. He instinctually knew every spot on my body that elicited a jolt straight through my core.

All thoughts fell out of my head when he placed my hands on the mattress and lifted my hips higher. A commanding knee pushed mine apart roughly. Smoke swirled around my head like incense with his intoxicating scent—I could come just by breathing it in.

The smoke thickened around us, and I smiled with satisfaction. He was losing control, and I was the cause. The thought of this magnificent male losing himself over me sent a thrill up my spine. "Mate with me, Káidyn," I coaxed.

He was big, and he took his time, working me up even more. By the time his broad head teased my entrance, I was already whimpering. I tried to move my hips back to meet him, desperate for his long, thick length to fill me, but his large hands gripped my hips tightly, holding me in place.

"Are you ready for me, moi vozlyublennyi?" he asked, his voice so guttural and otherworldly I could barely understand him. I got the message as he pushed into me slowly, inch by sweet, tortuous inch.

"God, yes! Please, Káidyn. More."

He rocked slowly. His tip dipping shallowly in and out of me in a tortuous rhythm. When the first ridge on his cock rubbed against my g-spot, my hands fisted the covers, and I let out a long, desperate groan into the mattress.

That noise seemed to snap something within him, and he slammed into me to the hilt. I screamed his name in sweet agony as he filled me completely, and he stilled. My back warmed as he leaned over me, consuming my entire body in his heat. "I love to hear you scream my name, my blood. I want every sound you make, my queen. But the harridan might return with your cries."

I bit my lip as his hands slipped around me and cupped my breasts, heavy and aching with need. I could do nothing but pant and swallow my groan with every touch of his skin on mine. Sweat beaded on my forehead, between my breasts, and down the small of my back from his fiery caresses. I shook with need and want. I was nearly feverish. Káidyn gave new meaning to "hot sex," and I loved every minute of it.

Setting me back on the mattress, he straightened behind me. Then he moved, retreating partially before thrusting back in. His large hands dug into my thighs as his pace quickened. My fists gripped the blankets as I braced, his thrusts growing stronger and more intense with each push.

His voice, deep and gravelly, was more dragon than man when he spoke in a near-chant. "So tight. So wet. So needy. My queen. My blood. My heart."

I bit my knuckles to keep from crying aloud at his relentless rhythm, the ridges of his natural Jacob's ladder making my eyes cross. The bed banged on the wooden floor in time with his fervor. Just as I approached the crest of another wave of rapture, his rhythm stuttered, and he roared. And then, I swear to sweet baby Jesus, fire shot over my shoulder.

Dewey hissed from the dresser, barely avoiding the flames. His tail may have been smoking—just a little but, honestly, I couldn't focus on that when my entire body ignited in bliss. Despite Káidyn's previous warning, I couldn't stop a scream of ecstasy. My vision blurred. I might have blacked out for a moment again.

When I regained consciousness, I found us tangled together on my bed. His incredible heat still pulsed within me, his cock throbbing as we clung to each other. I focused on simply breathing, my mind unable to process any rational thoughts. Finally, my synapses fired enough that low words being mumbled over and over in my ear began to make sense: "Mine. My mate. My blood. My queen. Mine."

Chapter Six

Reality Bites

The rest of Saturday and Sunday disappeared way too soon. Between occasional naps and snacking, we explored each other's bodies. Thoroughly. We couldn't seem to get enough of each other. I didn't quite understand the magical bond that connected us so deeply, but decided to not overthink it.

When dawn broke Monday morning, I was exhausted, but more sated and content than I'd ever felt in my life. Right Said Fred shocked us awake, and I smacked the alarm off. I groaned and tried to roll out of bed, but Káidyn's arm caught me around the middle and hauled me back to his chest.

"Mine," he mumbled sleepily.

I stroked the smooth, red scales that seemed to pop up whenever he said that. "I have to go to work, Káidyn."

He cracked open an eye and the pupil of his golden eye suddenly became thin and vertical. He blinked, and it returned to its usual round shape as he shifted onto an elbow and frowned at me. "I will accompany you."

"No, you will not," I huffed. "How would I explain a six-foot-six stranger with scales and, more importantly, functioning wings?

Besides, I wouldn't get any work done with you around, distracting me."

"I am very good at distracting you." His lips traced from the top of my shoulder to my breast, on their way to a nipple.

My skin erupted in goosebumps. "Nope, nope, nope!" I shimmied out from under him and stood. That was way too close. If he started on my breasts, I would have had no control at all. As it was, looking at him sprawled across my bed, his black hair mussed, and his wings slowly beating, had me clenching my thighs together against the uninhibited moisture.

His nostrils flared, and a wicked smile bloomed across his mouth. "Ah, you want me too, krov' moja." His talented tongue swiped around his lips and my knees went weak. I'd learned well what a special thing a dragon tongue was ... and what it could do.

I scowled. "Stop sniffing me." I pointed a finger at his mouth. "And stop doing that thing with your tongue."

His grin widened. "But you like the things I do with my tongue, my queen."

Retreating, I padded to the bathroom. "That doesn't matter. I have to go to work. There's no one to take over for me on such short notice," I shouted from the sink as I put toothpaste on my toothbrush.

He followed me, his large body taking up most of the space in the tiny room. "I don't approve. You would have me languish here while you serve lesser tasks and masters?"

He crossed his arms over his chest, making his biceps pop even more than normal. "That's unacceptable. I'm a king! You're my queen. You should not work. You should attend to my needs."

The petulant set of his sensual mouth made him look like a sulky toddler denied his favorite cookies. I rolled my eyes at my reflection as I finished brushing and rinsed my mouth. Even an all-powerful dragon lord had some things to learn about Twenty-first Century relationships, it seemed.

"Tell you what, Your Majesty," I said, turning to stroke his stubbled jaw and soothe the savage beast. "Let me go to work today and arrange a leave of absence. I'll tell them my, uh, exotic foreign beau is whisking me off on a surprise extended vacation. That'll buy us some time to figure this whole thing out, without leaving my friends and colleagues in the lurch."

Káidyn still looked mulish, but he turned his head to press a kiss to my palm. "If we must," he allowed begrudgingly. "But I mislike letting you out of my sight, mo ghrá. Who knows what dastardly villains or tempting wenches might try to waylay you?"

I shook my head, even as a little thrill went through me at his possessiveness. "Down, boy. I think I can manage a simple workday without being abducted by a mustache-twirling rival or throwing myself at the first scantily clad maiden I see."

Káidyn muttered something that sounded concerningly like, "You'd better not, or I'll raze this city to the bedrock," but nodded reluctantly as he stood and pulled on his skin-tight breeches. I wondered randomly when he'd last laundered them and whether he had more than the one pair.

"Fine. We are agreed. I shall accompany you to this place of indenture, to stand guard outside against any who might—"

"No way." I cut him off, placing both hands flat on his chest—his warm, hard, impossibly sculpted chest I could pet instead of heading to work ... I shook myself and took a step back.

"You are staying put, mister. The last thing I need is a jumbo-sized fire-breather with poor impulse control tromping around my nice, flammable library."

I grabbed his hand and tugged him into the living room, snagging my robe on the way so I wouldn't be naked while brewing coffee. "Here, you can keep yourself busy with the TV while I'm gone. Just think of it like a magic scrying screen showing stories from all over the world."

I clicked on the flatscreen and scrolled until I found a Batman movie marathon, hoping the masked vigilante's over-the-top schtick would appeal. Káidyn cocked his head, looking intrigued despite himself.

"Very well," he rumbled, sprawling on my secondhand couch in a way that did alarming things to my higher brain function.

Whoever decided gray sweatpants were sexy had never seen Káidyn in thin leather breeches. They left very little to the imagination and, despite our sexcapades all weekend, I could tell his desire had yet to wane. The sheer indecency of it was another reason I couldn't have him loitering outside the library, shocking little old ladies into heart attacks.

He studied the remote, fiddling with the volume buttons. "I shall study this 'teevee' and its tales of costumed mortal men. But hurry back to me, beloved. If you tarry overlong, I will come questing for you."

I shuddered to think of the havoc an over-anxious dragon shifter could wreak on an unsuspecting small town. Talk about a bull in a China shop. "Do not come questing for me before sundown. I'll be back before nightfall," I promised, bending to press a swift, hard kiss to his mouth before running back to my bedroom to shower and find something to wear that would cover my new tattoo.

A turtleneck would be uncomfortable but might be necessary. The tattoo crossed my back, went up my neck, and down my arms and legs. Surely, I had something with a nice high neck that wouldn't draw stares in summer. Five minutes of searching had me cursing the Texas heat. Nothing with a ruffly collar in sight.

Inspiration striking, I dug through my drawers until I came up with a large silk scarf my Aunt Cherie had given me, but I'd never worn due to its garish colors. After tying it at a jaunty angle, I surveyed my handiwork in the mirror. I still didn't like it, which was why I'd never worn the thing, but it'd have to do.

Slipping on my sensible black flats, I jogged through the living room and to the front door, flinging my messenger bag over my shoulder. Káidyn looked up, his eyes surveying me as he licked his lips. He stood and followed me so swiftly I took a couple of steps back on instinct. He prowled toward me, a haunting growl coming from his chest.

My back hit the front door and I froze. Our eyes met as he got close, resting his hands flat against the door next to my head. "Be good," I cajoled, "and I'll bring you back a burger and some hoard-building books." My voice sounded breathy and hungry even to myself, belying my nonchalant words.

Káidyn nipped at my bottom lip, eyes molten and promising wicked adventures before he stepped back and freed me from the cage of his arms. "Don't be cruel, temptress. Leave now, before I change my mind and ravish you over this coffee table."

Flushed and flustered, I nodded and fled out the door while I still could. The walk to work felt simultaneously long and short.

Every minute away from Káidyn felt agonizingly long. And yet, a few blocks' walk wasn't enough time for me to process everything that had happened since Friday.

An all-powerful, magical, stud muffin dragon king sprung to life from the pages of a borrowed novel and claimed me as his eternal mate? Check. The undeniable, supernatural bond between us tattooed across my skin like an interdimensional mating mark? Double check. I didn't really understand it, and my commute did little to help me parse out the mysteries of Káidyn and multiple dimensions. My degree in library sciences did not prepare me for the practical applications of quantum physics or whatever.

I was in so far over my head, I couldn't even see daylight.

Chapter Seven

Scenting the Trail

A s I climbed the library steps, I took a deep breath, trying to gather my scattered thoughts. I needed to focus on getting through the day without arousing suspicion or accidentally blurting out that I'd left a hot as fuck dragon shifter on my couch after spending a solid forty-eight hours mating. That was not a story for the polite company of library patrons.

I hurried inside, keeping my head down and my sleeves pulled low over the magical markings on my skin. The last thing I needed was someone spying the tattoos and starting a town-wide inquisition.

"Morning, Tessa," Mildred chirped as I failed to scurry past the circulation desk undetected. Talking to Mildred was a bad plan. That woman had the nose of a bloodhound and the tenacity of a honey badger when it came to ferreting out gossip.

I pasted on a bright smile, praying my cheeks weren't actually as red as they felt. "Hi, Mildred! Lovely day, isn't it? Well, better get cracking on those, uh, card catalogs ..."

"Not so fast, missy." Mildred pinned me with a keen, all-too-knowing look. "I've been around the block a time or two, and I know the look of a woman who's been thoroughly debauched by her one true love. Spill!"

I gaped at her, jaw hanging somewhere around my knees. "I ... you ... how ... what?"

Mildred cackled, eyes dancing with mischief. "Oh, don't act so scandalized. I wasn't born yesterday, you know. I've been waiting for this day for a long time."

She leaned in conspiratorially, voice dropping to a whisper. "You've been chosen, Tessa. Chosen by forces older and greater than you can possibly imagine. Your dragon king has finally found you, hasn't he?"

I felt the blood drain from my face. "How could you possibly know about that?" I croaked. My eyes darted around wildly to make sure no one was eavesdropping on this bizarre conversation.

Mildred smiled enigmatically. "Let's just say I have a sense for these things. The Sight and various other magics have been in my family for generations. We've served the Dragons for eons and long awaited the return of the Dragon King for his human queen."

She reached out and patted my cheek comfortingly. "Don't be afraid, dear. You were born for this. Trust in your dragon, and in your own heart. They won't lead you astray."

I shook my head, my eyes unfocused. Reality was slipping from my grasp. Dragons? Destiny? An ancient bloodline of seers masquerading as mild-mannered library volunteers?

It was too much. I needed to sit down. Or maybe knock back a stiff drink. Possibly both.

"Mildred," I said, measuring my words. "I appreciate the, uh, vote of confidence, but I think there's been some kind of mistake. I'm no queen, and I'm definitely not the chosen anything. I'm just a small town librarian who stumbled onto something way, way over my pay grade."

Mildred's eyes crinkled with a knowing smile. "We're all more than we appear, Tessa. Even you. Especially you. The magic chose you for a reason. Best you start believing in your own power."

She straightened, adjusting her cardigan primly. "Now, I do believe we both have work to be getting on with. But my door is always open if you need guidance, or a sympathetic ear. This adjustment can be overwhelming at first. And once you've settled, we have things to talk about."

"Right," I said weakly. "I'll, uh, keep that in mind. Thanks, Mildred."

As I ambled to my office in a daze, I thought I heard her chuckle softly under her breath. "Anytime, Your Majesty. Anytime."

Could this day get any weirder? On second thought, I decided not to tempt fate by asking.

By some miracle, I managed to make it through lunch without further earth-shattering revelations or metaphysical crises. The mysterious tattoos stayed quiet under my clothes, and if I was slightly more distracted and jittery than usual, my coworkers graciously didn't comment.

Then, just as I was starting to relax, all hell broke loose.

"Krov' moja!" A familiar voiced boomed from across the silence of the library, drawing me from my office. He called for me again at full volume, followed by a distinct feline yowl and several gasps.

Fuck. I speedwalked as fast as I could to the front of the building, throwing what I hoped were smiles that conveyed "nothing to see here" to the patrons, even while knowing the whole way that I was failing utterly at it.

Káidyn's entire face lit up when he saw me rushing around the circulation desk. "My beloved queen! There you are."

"Shh. Keep your voice down," I instructed, looking over my shoulders for gawkers or eavesdroppers. "I thought I told you not to come here. Why do you have Dewey? And what are you wearing?"

Even to my own ears, my voice sounded slightly hysterical despite the whispering. Káidyn shrugged and stroked Dewey's head. Her eyes closed and she purred so loud I wanted to shush her as well. Traitor.

"Your familiar ran out the door when I was leaving and refused to go back inside. Once we were a fair way down the street, she sat and allowed me to pick her up and carry her to you. She misses you as well."

He tugged on the hem of a hot pink T-shirt that read "Common Grounds Café" in a flowery script, but no amount of pulling would cover his midriff. How Káidyn stretched the shirt over his massive chest, I couldn't begin to imagine. At least his wings seemed to be tucked away, somehow. He made a face when his tugging caused the fabric to rip along the side seam under his arm. "This flimsy tunic was the only thing that stretched enough for me to don."

A heavy sigh escaped me. Rubbing my forehead where I could feel the headache starting to bloom, I asked, "How did you find me?"

Káidyn tapped the side of his nose. "You cannot hide from me, my love. I found you across dimensions, I can find you across a small town. Your succulent scent calls to me. I simply followed my nose."

He proceeded to rub said nose along my neck and inhaled deeply. An animalistic rumble vibrated from his chest, and I felt it all the way to my core. I had no control around this man—dragon king—whatever.

An instant later, Dewey was on the floor, and I was backed into the nearest stacks, slammed against a shelf. Several books tumbled to the floor as scorching lips claimed mine in a bruising, desperate kiss.

"I could not bear to be without you a moment longer," Káidyn growled against my mouth, hands already roving feverishly over my body, as if reassuring himself I was real. "Wretched woman, leaving me to count the seconds until your return. If you ever deprive me of your presence for so long again, I shall raze this city to cinders."

"Hey, easy there, Your Highness," I said when I could breathe again. "We talked about this, remember? Tessa work. Káidyn stay. No razing or cinder-izing necessary."

Káidyn made a disgusted noise deep in his throat, but his embrace gentled as he nuzzled into my neck. He was sniffing me again with that half man, half dragon nose of his. I tried desperately to remember if I'd used deodorant this morning. Too late now.

"As my queen commands," he rumbled begrudgingly. "But I mislike being parted from you, my peach. It makes my insides itch and my claws twitch."

Despite the Armageddon-adjacent implications of his words, my insides melted like marshmallow fluff in a s'more at the tender words of my terrifying, fire-breathing cinnamon roll.

"I missed you, too," I admitted, threading my fingers through his gloriously rumpled hair. "But I wasn't just lollygagging around, you know. I was laying the groundwork for us to figure out this whole dragon-mate situation."

Káidyn made an interested noise, head popping up like an eager puppy. "Oh? Do tell."

Just as I opened my mouth to tell him about what Mildred had said, the sneaky woman popped up on the other side of the bookshelf, her face peeking out between Minimalism for Maximalists and Hoarding for Beginners. "We need to have a chat, dear," she said in her bird-like chirp. When her eyes beheld Káidyn, she tipped her chin in a small bow. "Your Highness. It's a pleasure to meet you at long last."

Káidyn's eyes swirled gold and his nostrils flared. "Keeper," he responded, placing a fist over his heart.

My eyes darted back and forth between the pair. I wondered whether I would ever catch up, or if I would be confused forever. "Uh, you know Mildred?"

"No, but I recognize her line. They have a very distinctive scent."

I sniffed hesitantly, feeling weird about it. Mildred smelled like old books and Chanel No. 5, like she always did. That dragon nose was something else.

"Let's go to my office," I suggested, scooping up Dewey and herding the two of them out of the stacks and past tables of patrons, a maniacal smile plastered on my face. I'm sure it would be all over town by dinnertime that the librarian had a strange man in a hot pink crop top and carrying a cat to visit her.

Chapter Eight

The Notebook, Red Bull, And a Prophecy

I placed Dewey on my desk and she immediately settled in, grooming a back leg like she belonged there. I shut the door.

Before I could sit in my chair, Káidyn claimed it and pulled me into his warm (and distracting) lap. "Káidyn," I protested, squirming.

Mildred swatted a hand in my direction. "There's no sense fighting against the possessive nature of a dragon mate, my dear." Her red lips tipped up. "It's a battle you cannot win. Dragons are very territorial and supremely affectionate."

Affectionate was one word for it. Horny was another, more accurate, word. I stifled a giggle at the thought. Now was not the time for laughter. If I let loose, the hysteria rising in me might overwhelm me. Taking Mildred's advice, I gave up and sat back, definitely not noticing the hard muscles of Káidyn's chest and abdomen, or the hard length of him that was growing under my derrière.

"So, my dears, I've been speaking with my sister, and we seem to have somewhat of a kerfuffle on our hands." Mildred rested her hands on her knees and leaned forward.

"What is the problem, Keeper?" Káidyn's voice was steady and calm, but his hands on my body never quit moving. He drew circles on my back and stroked my shoulders. My dragon tattoo warmed and shifted under his touch. I shivered at the sensation, while trying hard to focus.

"Let me ask you a question first, Your Highness." Mildred looked pained. "How long have you been here, exactly?"

Káidyn's hands stilled as he thought. "Since the first hour of the day you call Saturday."

"About sixty-one hours then. I was afraid of that." Mildred tapped a finger on her lip.

I sat up straight, my attention refocused. "What do you mean? What are you afraid of?"

Mildred slapped her knees and stood. "No other answer for it then." She shook her head and gave me a sympathetic smile. "I hoped we'd have more time to ease you into this, Tessa dear, but with this particular spell and volume, we only have seventy-two hours and that's cutting it close. We really should strive to make it in sixty-eight, just in case."

"Sixty-eight hours for what exactly?" I hopped off Káidyn's lap and began to pace, barely controlling my spiking anxiety.

"To get you back to Emberfall, of course. The prophecy of the Dragon King and his human queen only has so long to be fulfilled." She snapped her fingers. "Keep up, dear."

"Excuse me, what? I thought 'queen' was just a term of endearment." I rubbed my sweaty palms on the front of my pants.

"I can't be a real queen, with queen responsibilities. I'm a librarian from Texas! Unless Emberfall is less than a forty-five-minute drive from my mom, I can't move there."

Without acknowledging my concerns, Káidyn stopped my pacing by standing behind me and resting his large hands on my shoulders. "And if we fail to make the deadline?"

Mildred frowned as she delivered the news. "Very bad things, I'm afraid, Your Highness. You will be unable to return, your kingdom will crumble, and your love will be destroyed."

I gasped. "I'll die?"

"No. Not you personally, my dear—your relationship. You see ..."

"Not possible," Káidyn interrupted. "Our bond cannot be broken." The heat emanating from his body increased in intensity, warming my backside to an uncomfortable degree.

Mildred tsked. "I hate to be the bearer of such news, Your Highness, but Myrna is very sure. She is High Keeper, and she's never wrong."

I tilted my head back, looking up at my dragon. His strong jaw worked, the muscles ticking. His eyes blazed and smoke wafted from his nostrils in a steady stream. I became mesmerized by the lines of his cheekbones dotted with stubble and the occasional flickering scale.

Noticing me staring, he glanced at me. He smiled softly, his eyes cooling to a delicate gold. He stroked my cheek with a knuckle. "What's the solution, Keeper? I will let nothing threaten my queen."

"Back in the book you go, of course." Mildred rifled through stacks on my desk and searching my office shelving. "Where is it?"

Fascinated by Káidyn's caresses, I nearly forgot Mildred was there. Blinking at her stupidly, I frowned. "Where is what?"

"The book, dear," she said with an exasperated sigh. "The book whence your dragon mate came."

"The book? Oh, it's at home, of course."

"Then let's go, my dears. No time to waste!"

"But Mildred, I can't leave the library unattended. I'm the only one on staff today."

"Leave that to me," she said quickly and grabbed the old-fashioned microphone off my desk. Flicking a switch, she announced: "Library patrons. Due to unforeseen circumstances, the library is closing early today. Please make your way to the circulation desk to check out your books immediately. Thank you." She set the microphone back on its perch. "C'mon. Let's close up and get out of here."

Káidyn scooped up Dewey, placing her on his beefy shoulder for her ride home. Dewey exploded with purrs as we followed Mildred out of my office. I rolled my eyes at them and trailed behind Mildred.

Káidyn barely fit on the bench seat of Mildred's ancient Chevy pickup. My mind stuttered along with the spark plugs as their intentions for when we reached my apartment sharpened in my mind. Dragon shifters, magical books, Keepers, kings and queens:

I was overwhelmed, and still a little concerned I might be deep in psychosis.

On the drive, Káidyn announced he was famished and required sustenance before any prophecies could be dealt with. We stopped at a Whataburger, and I ordered him a pile of cheeseburgers, because I feared a hangry dragon.

A few minutes later, I was turning the key in the lock to my front door when Káidyn asked Mildred, "Do we have time to bring this Netflix menace to heel? I hate to abandon my queen's homeland to this threat."

Before I could fathom what he meant, I opened the door, my jaw dropped, and our bags of food slipped from my fingers. Popcorn kernels, couch stuffing, and Red Bull cans punctured by claws littered every surface of the living room. The flat screen TV was on, paused on the emotional climax of The Notebook, of all things. In the middle of the floor sat a dragon-sized nest of pillows where Káidyn had obviously taken up residence while he was left alone this morning.

"My house! I don't ... you ... how ..." I sputtered, torn between bursting into hysterical laughter and tearing my hair out by the roots. "I was only gone for a few hours! How in the hell did you make such a mess? And what's this about Netflix needing to 'heel'? It's a streaming service, not an untrained mastiff. You're the true menace."

Káidyn crossed his burly arms, and honest-to-God pouted. "You underestimate the deviousness of this Netflix, my love. Clearly, it seeks to infiltrate our happy home and sow seeds of discord. Why, that fiendish, manipulative wench"—he gestured wildly at Rachel McAdam's tear-streaked face frozen on the screen—"made a mockery of the sacred bond between mates! Cavorting with scrawny, weak-chinned human suitors when she clearly belongs with her brooding, passionate beloved. It's a travesty!"

I opened and closed my mouth a few times, absolutely no sound coming out, like a fish on a hook. Finally, I squeaked, "The Notebook is fiction. Made up. For entertainment purposes. You get that, right?"

Káidyn's brow furrowed. "Explain. Do you mean Netflix are players, putting on a mummer's farce for the masses?"

I sighed. My dragon had a few gaps in his education. I rescued our dinner from the floor. "Why don't we eat while I walk you through the finer points of Twenty-First Century culture? We're going to have to seriously calibrate your understanding before you accidentally try toppling governments or challenging Ryan Gosling to a duel."

Káidyn sniffed disdainfully, but the tantalizing scent of burgers was already pulling his attention. "I am hungry. I suppose you can teach me your Netflix culture while you feed me."

"No time, dears," Mildred announced from behind us, making me jump. I was so focused on Káidyn I forgot she was with us. "It's not important right now. There won't be any Netflix where you are going, anyway."

Káidyn made a grumpy noise of assent, already elbow-deep in cheeseburgers. "You'll have plenty of time to tell me about your strange customs when we are back at Emberfall, my love."

My heart turned over at the satisfied rumbles and slurps emanating from his general direction. I sighed. This crazy, impossible male was now mine, faults and world domination threats included. And I was his, magical tattoos, romance books, entitled felines, and all. We were stuck with each other. And, somehow, I was fine with that.

Chapter Nine

Fairy Tale Endings

As Káidyn demolished an entire bag of cheeseburgers and I picked at my fries, Mildred explained what we would have to do to fulfill the prophecy, save his kingdom, and preserve our love.

"You're not eating, my queen?" Káidyn offered me a cheeseburger that I declined.

"I've lost my appetite," I answered lamely. How could I eat when Mildred just told me that I would have to leave my home, my life, everything I've ever known, to go live in a book? "I'm feeling ... I don't know. Nervous, I guess."

Káidyn wiped his perfect mouth and flashed me a smile. "Do not be nervous, my beloved! My people will rejoice greatly to meet their prophesied queen. There shall be grand feasts, and balls, and all manners of celebrations to welcome you. The people of Emberfall will love you almost as much as I do."

I gulped at the thought, and Káidyn's eyes watched my throat bob. "And then, moi vozlyublennyi, the things I'm going to do to you ... Epic poets will compose odes to our passion for centuries to come."

I flushed hot all over, suddenly very aware of the dragon-sized bulge straining the placket of his breeches. Good gravy, had it only been this morning when he tumbled me against the wall and rocked my world right off its axis? It felt like a lifetime ago.

Responding to my body's very unsubtle cues, Káidyn rose fluidly to his feet and circled the coffee table. He moved sinuously, prowling towards me, golden eyes gleaming. Suddenly, the circular pupils changed, elongating into the sharp, vertical slits of a giant reptile.

The transformation was swift yet mesmerizing, like watching the gradual, deliberate constriction of a camera's aperture. The sclera surrounding the pupils darkened, taking on an almost metallic sheen, while the irises brightened into a vibrant, molten gold reminiscent of the gleam of a predator's gaze in the dark.

I gulped again, this time in anticipation rather than apprehension.

"I've been more than patient, my queen." He pulled me up from the floor and pressed me tightly along his hard, muscled body. "I let you go to your human job, even though you are above such common things, and didn't torch anyone who looked at you. I'd say I've earned a reward. Don't you agree?"

"What kind of reward did you have in mind?" My voice sounded sultry, confident and sexy in a way that was new for me. Desire and anticipation bled together in a heady rush as I came alive in his arms.

One hand caught my hip, the other tangling in my hair to tip my head back. His face inches from mine, Káidyn's eyes burned into me, savage and adoring. "You are so beautiful. You are a goddess," he rasped. "I will never tire of this sight," he rumbled, voice rough with want. "I'm going to take you apart, sweet mate. Pleasure you until you forget your own name, until the only word you remember is mine. And then I'm going to put you back together again and start all over. I won't stop until the only reality you know is me moving inside you. Claiming you. Loving you."

Holy mother of God! I think my ovaries actually exploded.

A throat cleared, and a chirping voice cut through the fog of my lust. "Not that I'm against young love and all that, but we do have business to attend to, dears. Time is running short."

My entire body heated with embarrassment as I took in the old woman's smug smile. I gave Káidyn's chest a little push, but it did exactly nothing. Kissing my head, he turned me to face Mildred, but held me close. My mind cleared a bit more, and I remembered my anxiety. I trembled in Káidyn's strong arms, and I found my voice.

"Káidyn, I need you to be patient a little longer because we need to talk. I can't leave everything and everyone I know and love behind for sex—even mind-blowing sex. I need true love, purpose, a life besides attending to your needs. You are asking a lot from me, and I've only known you three days."

Káidyn smiled. "This is why you're my queen. No woman in my realm would ever be bold enough to speak so plainly with me. You are extraordinary."

"I'm an average, normal human woman," I demurred. "Pretty plain, really."

He took my hand and brought me to the sofa. "Sit, my love."

Once I was comfortable, he blew magic smoke from his nose until it wrapped my head in a cloud. It filled my nose with its heady scent. I sighed and breathed deeply.

"Close your eyes."

I obeyed, swept away by the scent of the ocean breeze. My skin warmed. "Káidyn, I feel like I'm on a tropical island." I couldn't remember the last time I'd taken a vacation, and I'd never been anywhere interesting. I was thirty, and I'd never been anywhere, nor had any adventures. Before I could feel too sad about it, though, Káidyn's voice broke into my reverie.

"I know you. I felt you across dimensions. My soul recognizes your soul, and nothing will keep me from you." He wrapped me in a cocoon of his wings, like when he claimed me on Saturday morning. "You have doubts because you don't recognize our soul bond yet and we must take the time to rectify this. Clear your mind and let me in."

The tattoo marking my back and limbs warmed and began to move. The dragon crawled around my skin like a caress. As it did, I felt weightless, like I was flying, or floating. The ecstasy of a love unlike any I'd ever known expanded from inside my chest until it reached every cell in my body.

And, most extraordinarily of all, I saw Káidyn in my mind, as though we were in a dream. I saw him hatching. I saw him as a child, playing with his brothers and sisters. I saw him sitting on his throne as a thoughtful and compassionate king who would burn to ash anyone who threatened his people.

He downloaded everything about him straight into my heart. Every laugh and every moment of joy. Every heartbreak, every challenge, and every disappointment. I saw all his courage and heroic acts. And it filled me with a deep appreciation of the extraordinary man—dragon—he was.

I saw, and felt, his loneliness, his desire for the companionship of a partner he could always rely on, and his wish for children. (I really feared for my ovaries at that last part. I swear, they were vibrating in my lower belly, ready to ovulate all the eggs.)

I also saw how he searched tirelessly for me, and the love I felt intensified. A golden light from my dragon tattoo became so bright it blinded me. But I didn't need to see, because I felt his fire drawing me close and making me safe. Then my soul recognized his soul, making me gasp.

It was so beautiful. "Káidyn," I cried, reaching for him, needing his physical embrace before I floated away forever on the blissful golden light.

Wrapping me in his arms, Káidyn's rich voice filled my ears like a meditation. "Tessa, my heart. Do you remember what you said when you blew out your birthday candle?"

"I wished for excitement," I said. "I wished for romance and adventure. I wished for the unexpected."

"Your wish came true," he said. "You will have all those things, and more. Take the leap. You won't regret it."

I smiled, my mind made up. "Okay. But only if I can bring Dewey. I've made a lifelong commitment to her that I have to honor."

"Of course, my heart. I wouldn't dream of leaving Dewey behind." And with that, he tucked his wings away, the smoke dissipated, and we were embracing on the sofa in my living room.

Mildred ate popcorn from Dewey's armchair, watching us with a gleam in her eye. "Are you two lovebirds ready to go?"

I smiled at her sheepishly and nodded.

Káidyn stood and pulled me back to my feet. "Speak, Keeper. What must we do first?"

Mildred set the book on the coffee table and spoke to Káidyn in a language I couldn't decipher.

My heart fluttered like a hummingbird. "What are you saying?"

"There's no translation," Mildred explained. "You'll learn the language soon enough."

I worried my hands. "What about my mom?" I pushed hair behind my ears. "I mean, I know she's a nosey body and I'm thirty years old, but, well, I'm all the family she has since we lost my dad."

Mildred's sharp blue eyes softened, and she patted my cheek. "Don't worry about Sharon, my dear. Myrna or I will send her along shortly."

"You can do that? Wait. She doesn't have a fated dragon mate, too, does she?" My eyes widened as a smug smile spread across Mildred's face. "Oh my God, she does, doesn't she? She's going to flip out! She told me last week that she's finally ready to try dating again."

Káidyn chuckled and wrapped me in his arms once again. "I look forward to meeting your mother soon."

"Ready then?" Mildred asked, glancing at the thin gold Timex on her wrist.

I nodded and leaned back into Káidyn's arms.

"Oh, I almost forgot." With a swipe of Mildred's hand, a beautiful ruby red gown replaced my simple work clothes and ugly scarf. My fingers and neck dripped with gold. Reaching a hand to my head, I grazed a crown, which I knew was gold without having to look at it. I smoothed my other hand over the luscious velvet of my dress, appreciating that it was the fanciest dress I'd ever worn.

"I don't know how you did that, but thank you, Mildred. I'll miss you terribly." My vision blurred with gathering tears.

"Don't cry, dear. You never know where an old lady might pop up." She winked.

Mildred lifted her hands over her head and the blissful golden light surrounded us. Intense pressure and a sudden tugging sensation made me panic. "Dewey!" I screamed, but by then my one-bedroom apartment and all I had ever known blinked out of view, and I was in Emberfell with Káidyn.

Picking up the red leather tome from the coffee table, the old Keeper studied the cover and smiled. For where once a handsome dragon king had flown all alone, now he sat on a golden throne, his queen beside him smiling beatifically ... and a very regal cat sitting on his lap.

Epilogue

Two weeks later ...

In a daze of lust, I let Káidyn walk me backward into our bedroom, shedding clothes with wild abandon along the way. By the time the backs of my knees hit the grand mattress with the silk and velvet coverlet, we were both bare and panting. The heat of my dragon king's gaze on my body was like a physical caress, searing and possessive.

"Goddess, look at you," he rasped. His breaths came in short pants of intoxicating smoke. "I will never tire of this sight. My woman, my mate, flushed and aching. Those lush curves begging for my hands and mouth. So beautiful. So perfect. And all mine."

"You say that all the time," I reminded him, my fingers entwining through his tousled raven hair.

"And I mean it all the time." And then he was on me, hot skin and rough hands and greedy kisses. I arched to meet him, sighing in relief as his large frame covered mine, the rightness of his weight on me zinging through my veins like lightning.

Káidyn took his time with me, proving good on every filthy promise he made since we arrived in Emberfall. Calloused fingers dancing over sensitive skin, clever tongue following every dip and hollow. He played my body like a maestro, coaxing shivery gasps and sobbing moans, stoking the fire higher and higher until I was delirious with need.

"Káidyn," I fairly whimpered, writhing against him shamelessly. "Please ... I can't ... I need ..."

"Shh. I know everything your body needs." Shifting his hips, he notched himself at my entrance, hard as steel and hot as a brand. "I've got you, mate. Brace yourself ..."

In one powerful surge, he was inside me to the hilt, stretching me open, reaching places I didn't know I could reach. I keened at the exquisite invasion, my fingernails scrabbling at his straining back. The slick drag of him, in and out, slow and deep, was unbearably good. He filled me utterly, physically and metaphysically, that magical soul-deep connection flaring as bright as a supernova.

"Yes," he gritted out, hips rolling in a dulcet rhythm as old as time. "Yes, Tessa, feel it. How perfectly you take me. How our bodies know each other, even as our souls twine tighter with every stroke. My queen, my goddess, my everything."

He punctuated each endearment with a grinding thrust, swiveling and retreating, only to plunge back even harder. I held on for dear life, reduced to soundless cries as he split me open and ruined me for all other men, not that there could ever be anyone else.

Káidyn dipped his head to claim my lips again, drinking my ecstatic sobs like wine. "That's it, máiteas," he panted against my open mouth. "Take all of me. Let me feel you fall apart on my cock."

His dirty mouth pushed me over the edge, and I came like a skyrocket, back arching clear off the bed as I clamped down on his pistoning length. Káidyn roared his approval, pounding into me harder, chasing his own release. Once, twice, three times, and then he was flooding me with liquid heat, my name a broken prayer on his lips.

For long moments, we rocked together, wringing out every last tremor and aftershock. Finally, he collapsed heavily on top of me, heedless of the mess, nuzzling into my neck with a contented rumble.

"Mmm ... I take back what I said about this realm being perplexing," I slurred, sleepy, boneless, and as sated as a jungle cat in a sunbeam. "Any dimension that has you in it is paradise to me."

"Ah, my lovely, I concur," he murmured fondly, pushing back his sweat-damp hair. My heart felt three sizes too big for my chest. It was so full of love and wonder and sheer incandescent happiness, I thought it might burst.

Less than a month ago, I'd been a bored librarian longing for adventure, for something beyond my humdrum routine. Now I was a dragon's mate, a queen, with newly discovered magic in my veins and a whole new world unfolding before me.

Sure, there were hurdles and learning curves. Integrating into a kingdom without cars, Doordash, or Netflix was bound to come with some bumps. But with Káidyn by my side, I felt like I could take on anything. Even if that anything was learning to ride a horse, embroider, or heat water with my budding magic.

Sensing the direction of my thoughts, Káidyn lifted his head to favor me with an indulgent grin. "What devious notions are spinning behind those pretty eyes, my love? More machinations to keep me from my solemn duties as protector of the realm?"

I snorted, tweaking his ear. "I think you've smited everyone that needs smiting for the moment. I was marveling at how life can change so quickly. My entire existence was thoroughly upended. I mean, dragons? Destiny? Magical kingdoms? It's a lot for a small town girl to wrap her head around."

Káidyn propped himself up on one elbow, tracing the curve of my cheek with a gentle caress. "I know it must seem overwhelming at times, máiteas. But I swear to you, on my honor as Dragon King, I will move heaven and earth to ensure your happiness. You will want for nothing, and fear nothing, so long as I draw breath."

He sealed his vow with a sweet, lingering kiss that curled my toes.

"In fact," he said as we parted, a wicked glint sparking in his eyes, "I think we're long overdue for a proper claiming flight. What better way to ease you into your new reality than a romantic moonlit cruise above the clouds?"

I gulped, suddenly envisioning clinging to Káidyn's scaled back as we zoomed through the troposphere. "Uh, yay? Wow, would you look at the time, I just remembered that Cook really needed me in the—"

"Oh no you don't!" Káidyn laughed, scooping me up in a princess carry and striding for the balcony. "No more excuses, my dragon queen. Your king demands your undivided attention. I promise you'll love it. I intend to make you come over and over above the clouds. In the sky, you can be as loud as you wish without fear of harridans."

With a roguish wink, he launched us into the night sky, his wings beating the air into submission as we rose. My shrieks of mingled alarm and delight trailed behind us like a banner.

I couldn't believe my little voice told me to be careful what I wished for. Screw that. I laughed as the cool night wind whipped color into my cheeks and my dragon's strong arms banded around me. The shimmering world spread out below us like a jeweled carpet as we rose higher and higher.

My last coherent thought as we shot into the star-strewn heavens, Káidyn's triumphant roar filling my ears, was I would never doubt the power of books again.

You know, just a typical Friday night. All part of the Dragon Queen gig.

Watch out, world. This small town librarian's happily ever after was about to get real.

The End

More from Dallas Ryan

If you need more sexy shifters and the women who tame them, check out Dallas' other work here:

https://linktr.ee/dallasryanwrites

Dallas Ryan, "The Queen of Feels," is a multi-genre author and nurse living in Virginia. When not writing emotionally charged stories, she creates yarn colors and enjoys margaritas. Follow her on Facebook or join her reader group, Dallas' Darlings.

Hard Up by Jayelle Dee

A Vibro-Shifter Romance

When love is trapped, you must set it free.

Vicki's gifted a used golden dildo with one speed. When it starts working on its own, she knows there is something supernatural going on. A mystery unfolds leading her down the rabbit hole of a curse, a jilted lover, and a beautiful man who needs her help.

Contents

Chapter One

The Gift

V icki's head jolted up as soon as the singing started.

"Happy birthday to you ..."

"Shit."

"Happy birthday to you!"

"Dammit."

Her coworkers rounded the hall and gathered at her cubical opening. She pivoted and gave her best surprised face, along with a smile.

"Happy birthday, dear Vicki! Happy birthday to you!"

Lina, the office party planner and Nosey McNoserton, leaned in with a cake. "I know you didn't want us to do anything, but you know I simply couldn't live with myself if we didn't do something."

Vicki waved a hand at her. "It's fine, Lina. It's very sweet of you. All of you." She stood and indicated towards a glass-walled room in the center of the cubicles. "Come on, everyone. I guess we're having cake in the conference room." Honestly, she couldn't complain. It was a nice gesture, and Lina meant well.

As Vicki shoved a piece of red velvet cake with cream cheese icing into her mouth, Lina handed her a cup of coffee.

"Why do you hate birthdays?" she asked in her usual probing tone.

"I don't hate birthdays," Vicki told her. "I just got dumped. Don't feel much like celebrating."

"Oh, I see. Well, I'm sorry to hear that. His loss, am I right?" Lina snort-laughed.

Vicki cringed inwardly, but made a display of giggling.

When the day was finally over, Vicki couldn't wait to get home, so she could spend the night with her vibrator and a bottle of wine. As soon as she walked through the door of her house, she changed into yoga pants and an oversized sweatshirt, and turned on the TV. Sipping wine straight from the bottle, she scrolled through Netflix.

A knock sounded on the door of her townhouse. "What the?" Vicki sat the wine down and looked through the peephole of her front door. Her best friend, Amy, stood there.

Vicki opened the door. "What are you doing here?"

"Interrupting your sulking, like any good friend would do. Happy birthday." She presented Vicki with a wrapped box."

Vicki's shoulders slumped, grateful for her friend's effort. Even though she wasn't in the mood to celebrate, everyone around her insisted on it. "Aww, Amy, you shouldn't have."

"I know. Can I come in or what?"

"Oh, yeah." Vicki walked back to her living room couch and plopped down.

Amy closed the door and joined her.

"He didn't deserve you, ya know," she said, setting the gift on the coffee table next to the wine bottle. She eyed the bottle. "Got one of those for me?"

"In the wine fridge. Take your pick."

Amy sauntered into the small open kitchen behind the living room. "Is this red velvet?" she called.

"Yep. Lina strikes again. Help yourself if you want some." Vicki continued scrolling through movie thumbnails.

Amy appeared with her own bottle of wine and a plate of cake. She sat on an over-stuffed chair next to the couch. She set her wine down on the coffee table and shoveled cake into her mouth. "Ya gonna open it?"

"Nope."

Amy guffawed. "Ohhhpehhhn eeeeet!"

A chortle bubbled from Vicki. "Fine! God!" A grin spread up her cheeks, despite herself. She tossed the remote and grabbed the bright package. "This better not be expensive."

"It wasn't cheap." Amy spoke with her mouth full.

"You really shouldn't have."

"Oh, come on. So, you lost 200 pounds of asshole a couple of weeks ago. That's no reason not to celebrate yourself."

Vicki nodded begrudgingly. "Yeah. You're right." She tore into the bright paper. "You got me a pair of Sketchers?"

"No. That's just the box it was shipped in."

Vicki opened the lid. Under a crumpled mass of tissue paper was the most beautiful, anatomically perfect gold sculpture of a six-inch penis. "Wow!" She laughed. "That's um ... really something. I got rid of an asshole, so you got me a dick?""Mm, not just any dick." Amy put down her plate. "This is special." She reached in and pulled out the shiny cock.

"It looks a little limp."

Amy snorted, rotated it, and presented it to Vicki. "See?"

Vicki looked at the base of the sculpture. There was a button. "Oh, my hell, is that a vibrator?"

Amy grinned. "It is! But look how realistic it is!"

Vicki took it from her, examining it. "I know. It's kinda creepy." She wiggled it in the air. The dildo was floppier than any she'd seen before. "It looks like solid gold, but feels squishy like silicone."

"Turn it on. Turn it on!" Amy begged.

Vicki complied. The large mushroom head and shaft buzzed and wiggled to life. The two of them howled with laughter, watching the flaccid fake penis flapping and humming. Vicki quickly turned it off.

"I can't—" she tried talking through her laughs. "That's hilarious!" Then she ran the tip of her finger along it and gripped it. "Wow. I mean, if I was blindfolded, I'd swear this was a real cock."

"I know, right?"

Vicki turned it on again. Pressing the button only turned it on and off. "Only one speed? No patterns or anything?""No, unfortunately. The chick I bought it from said it was very old."

"Ew! It's used?" Vicki dropped it in horror, and it flopped onto the coffee table.

Amy cackled. "It's a one-of-a-kind custom piece."

Vicki wrinkled her nose. "It's fucking used!"

"Don't be such a prude. Just clean it with some rubbing alcohol or something."

"You are disgusting."

Amy buckled over, laughing. "You don't have to use it. I just thought it was funny. And it's really pretty!"

Vicki picked it up again, examining it. It fascinated her how anatomically correct it was. She tossed it back in the box. "I'm not sure how much use I'll have for a limp dildo with one speed."

Amy pulled the golden phallus out of the box and set it back on the coffee table. "Maybe it's the flabby jiggling that gets you off?"

Vicki sarcastically arched a brow, studying it. "It really is cool looking. Thanks, Amy. I didn't mean to be ungrateful."

Chapter Two

The Surprise

A my had stayed and watched a movie with her then went home. After Amy left, Vicki decided to watch another movie and finish off the bottle of wine her friend had opened. Why not? It was her birthday, after all, and it was Friday. She could afford to sacrifice Saturday to a hangover.

May as well finish off her day with a one-woman party, even if she couldn't get laid. She didn't need a man to have fun. Most of the time, pleasing herself with her hand or a toy was better than the sex she had with her ex-boyfriend, anyway.

A steamy romance caught her eye, and she clicked on it. As it started, she grabbed a large piece of red velvet cake. Sugar and alcohol sounded like the perfect dinner. Tomorrow, she'd satiate herself with a giant burrito smothered in green chili from the Mexican place across the street.

Returning to the couch, she made herself comfortable, leaning back and drawing her legs up to her side. She drew her finger across the white cream cheese frosting on the surface of the cake, leaving a deep swipe as the frosting gathered on her fingertip. She plunged it into her mouth and sucked.

"Mmm," she moaned. "God, I love cream cheese icing. If cum tasted this good, I'd suck dick for days." She ate the cake with her hands. By the time she'd finished licking every morsel from her fingers, the movie was into its first sex scene.

Vicki watched the lead male character caressing the breasts of the lead female. Close ups of their kissing mouths, and his lips along her nipples awoke a pulse in her clit. She set the plate down and dove her hand into her yoga pants.

On the TV, a perfectly formed, muscular man dove into the supple body of the woman. Vicki's hand pressed and fondled her swelling clitoris. Pleasure welled through her body. By the time the characters on the screen were making their 'O' faces, she was nearly to her own climax. But she just couldn't get it to erupt. She rewound the movie and tried again, watching the characters' bodies writhing against each other.

She pressed and jiggled, pinched and flicked. A small moan escaped her. She was so close, and her frustration mounted. Why couldn't she get her bean off? Too much wine? Too frustrated? Not turned on enough? It was maddening!

Then her eye caught a glint of gold from the coffee table. The once flaccid dildo was erect. She yanked her hand from her pussy and sat upright.

"What the?" She stared at it. It was longer by nearly two inches, too. *Did that thing get hard?* Hesitantly, she reached for it. She stretched out her index finger, still wet from her own arousal, and poked it. It wobbled slightly. When she worked up the courage to pick it up, it felt exactly like an aroused penis in her grasp. Firm, but pliant.

"This is crazy," she murmured to herself. Still, she did love the feeling of a hard cock inside her. And she was just drunk enough from the wine ... "Fuck it, why not?" Vicki rose from the couch and took the dildo to the bathroom to clean it.

After some rubbing alcohol and soap and water, she toweled it off and returned to her living room. She pulled off her yoga pants and panties, plopped down on the couch, and hitched one leg up while letting the other dangle to the floor. A nice way to spread herself for pleasure.

She held the golden phallus at eye-level and examined it closely. The texture was incredible. Resembling the smoothness of tight skin. There were even subtle veins sweeping through it. She wrapped her other hand around its girth and squeezed. It responded with a slight pulse. Immediately she flung it, shouting, "Shit!"

Sitting up again, she regarded it on the floor. Hesitantly, she picked it up again. "What are you?" Tentatively exploring it with her fingertips, she pressed the tip between her thumb and forefinger. It was spongy, exactly like the crown of a real dick. "Maybe some kind of new AI tech? But Amy said it was really old. Huh."

Fascinated, she pressed the button on its base. The golden flesh hummed to life, and the tip wriggled so fast she could barely see it.

"Wow. That seems faster than the last time I turned you on." Her clit reminded her that she was horny with a deep throb. Resuming her previous relaxed posture on the couch, she spread herself and carefully approached her opening with the buzzing penis.

The moment it touched her slick, aroused slit, the most delicious pleasure shimmied through her.

"Oh my God!" She pushed it up towards her clit. The intensity of the sensation almost made her come right away. "Fuck." She slid it down, dragging it delicately along her labia, then rimmed her opening. The vibrating cock seemed to get warmer and firmer in her hand. "Jesus, how big does this thing get?"

Without need for much pressure, the cock slid inside her. Vicki moaned loudly as the penis plunged and retracted almost without her effort to move it. It felt huge inside her, filling her and hitting every hotspot perfectly. Her breaths quickened to handle her impending orgasm. She wanted it on her clit again, and pulled it out of her, pressing the tip firmly into her swollen nub. The climax happened immediately. Shockingly hard spasms rocked her body, and she squealed.

As her body relaxed, the dildo slid on its own back into her vagina for a few more thrusts, making her climax a second time.

"Oh, God! Jesus! Fuck!" Vicki wailed, clutching the fabric of the couch so hard she nearly ripped it. It was after her second orgasm, and her body calmed, when she realized she hadn't been holding the dildo.

Heaving breaths, she raised her head and looked at the base of it protruding from her cooch. And even stranger, it had stopped vibrating on its own, like it was also done.

"I'm not gonna freak out. I am *not* going to freak out." Forcing herself to be calm, she pulled the dick from her. It slid out, limp again in her hand. She sat up, inspecting it. "I need to ask Amy who she bought this from."

The next morning, Vicki couldn't wait to try the golden dildo again. Although she didn't understand why, it was the best toy she'd ever used. But last night could have been a fluke. After all, she'd revved her engines pretty hard before using it. She rolled over and retrieved it from the nightstand drawer where she'd placed it last night when she went to bed. It was already hard.

"Wow! Morning wood, I see." She snickered. Switching it on, she laid on her back and sent its delightful vibrating crown to her labia and smoothed it in a slow circle. She got aroused quickly as the vibrations seemed to penetrate her to her very core. She easily moistened the swollen tip with her slick wetness, dipping inside like a quill in an ink well to write waves of pleasure on her swelling clitoris. Its firmness, girth, and length grew as it warmed and pulsed against her.

"God, this thing is magic," she sighed. An orgasm took her, and she bucked her hips, screaming and gasping. The vibrator left her grasp and plunged inside her vagina, thrusting against a G-spot until she couldn't breathe from the spasms.

"Goddamn, you're amazing," she said, panting and recovering. It slipped out of her and laid limp between her thighs.

She played with the golden vibrator all weekend. She'd never been so horny. The gilded penis was better than any boyfriend. It was always ready, always hard, always got her off, and never complained about anything or farted.

Monday morning came too soon, as it always did. As Vicki arrived at work, she realized with disdain that the highlight of her birthday weekend was masturbating. But she had nothing else better to do. Friends had invited her out, but she wasn't in the mood. So many things reminded her of her ex. Except the golden vibrator. It satisfied her way more than he ever had.

As she walked past Lina's cubicle, the woman's annoying voice ring out.

"There she is! How was your birthday weekend, Vicki?"

Vicki cringed. Saying she'd spent the weekend masturbating with a magic dildo that made her come harder than any man seemed like something she shouldn't say to a coworker. "It was fine."

Lina's head popped over her gray partition like a gopher. "That's it? Just fine?"

Vicki halted and regarded her. "Yes. Just, fine. I did exactly what I wanted to. Watched TV, gorged on Mexican food, and drank wine."

"Oh. Well, I guess if I'd just gotten dumped, I'd do the same thing." Lina had the tact of a rhino.

Vicki stopped herself from scowling at Lina and continued to her own cubicle. When she got to her desk, Vicki turned on her computer and grabbed her cell phone to text Amy.

Vicki: Do you have any information on the seller of that birthday present you got me?

Amy: I remember her name is Rhonda. I think I still have her email. She's in Vermont. Why?

Vicki: Just interested in getting some info on it. It's so unique!

Amy: You used it, didn't you!

Vicki hesitated. Not like she and Amy didn't have some detailed conversations in the past, but she felt uncomfortable talking about this.

Vicki: We can talk later.

Amy: We better!

Amy texted an email address. Vicki couldn't wait and immediately pulled up her personal email on her phone.

> *"Dear Rhonda,*
> *"My name is Vicki, and my friend recently purchased*
> *a very unique ..."*

Dildo? Vibrator?

"... penis sculpture from you. I was curious about its origins. Any information you can share about this interesting item would be greatly appreciated. Thank you!"

That night, when she got home, Vicki saw her golden phallus laying on her coffee table, like it was waiting for her. "Hi, Goldwyn," she greeted, pulling off her shoes. Yes, she'd named it. Vicki bent down and patted it like it was a puppy.

"Ready for more fun tonight?" She went up the stairs to her bedroom and changed out of her work clothes into a long nightshirt. The plan for the night was dinner and watching another romantic movie with her vibrator.

In the kitchen, she started boiling water for spaghetti and checked email on her phone. There was a response from Rhonda. Vicki's stomach bounced.

"Dear Vicki,

I don't know much about it. It was my great aunt's. She was kind of an eccentric old lady who dabbled in spirituality and witchcraft. She had all kinds of weird stuff around her house. Anyway, she recently passed away, and this was among the things we found under her bed. I almost threw it away, but there was just something about it. I guess I thought it was special for some reason. I put it up on E-Bay. You never know what people will buy. No offense. Glad you like it."

Vicki read it again. "Huh. Witchcraft? Maybe it's enchanted or something?" She chuckled. "That's ridiculous. Witchcraft is nonsense. Well, okay, then. Guess I'm getting the best sex of my life from some random old lady's vibrator. There are worst things, I suppose." She decided not to overthink it and finished making dinner.

Vicki sat at her buffet counter between the kitchen and living room twirling noodles onto a fork. She'd brought Goldwyn over and set him on the counter across from her.

"So, you come from an old lady, huh? That had to suck. Having to work that dried out old snatch?" She chewed her pasta, then thought maybe she was being cruel. "I'm sorry. I shouldn't say that. Maybe she was really nice. Anyway, you're mine now."

When dinner was done, she picked up her prized phallus and sashayed to the living room. "Come on, Goldwyn, let's dance!"

Chapter Three

The Obsession

For two weeks, Vicki repeated the same ritual when she got home from work. She even started bringing Goldwyn into the Kitchen and chatted to him while she cooked dinner. She told her golden dick about her day, gossiped about her friends and coworkers, and even prattled about events in the news. Then she'd bring him to the living room for a movie and a dip in her love cave.

Vicki struggled to think of any other time in her life when she'd been so content. The routine she'd developed with her lovely golden penis made her happy. But by the end of the second week, she was starting to realize it was a little strange. Maybe she should take a break from it?

The thought of missing the incredible orgasms and vigorous penetration of her Goldwyn left her feeling empty. She needed it. Even though it was only a large dick, she'd never felt so well cared for before.

When Friday night came, Amy texted her to go out, but Vicki didn't want to. She'd rather spend the night with ... *Maybe this is becoming a little unhealthy.* She accepted Amy's invitation and met her at a dance club.

Vicki donned her favorite shiny, skin-tight, white mini-dress. It always looked stellar under black lights. Dangerously high platformed heels and large, sparkly earrings completed her look. She swept her dark locks up into a clip and applied false eyelashes over her brown eyes. The glow from all the amazing orgasms had her feeling super sexy, and she wanted it to show.

She walked into the club. Brightly colored lights flashed to the beat of pumping music. Bodies jumped and writhed on the dancefloor. Vicki spotted Amy at the bar and joined her.

"Yay!" squealed Amy, throwing her arms around her. "They're having two-for-one shots!" she shouted over the music.

"Perfect! Kamikaze!" Vicki yelled at the bartender.

Amy sized up Vicki. "You look incredible!"

Vicki grinned. "Thanks! I feel incredible!"

"I mean it! You're practically glowing!"

"It's the black lights!"

"No. YOU are glowing! Like you're in love!"

Vicki blushed. Who knew several nights full of toe-curling climaxes could make her look more attractive?

"So, what's going on?" demanded Amy.

"Nothing! Same old shit." Vicki accepted two shots from the bartender.

"Victoria, I know when you're lying to me. Seriously, what's going on?"

"Nothing! I swear."

Amy's eyes suddenly widened, and her eyebrows flew up. She focused on something behind Vicki. "Scorpio on your six."

Vicki gradually turned around and saw a tall, incredibly hot man standing behind her. He flicked his head, sending a long brown lock of hair flying over his shoulder. Brown eyes, chiseled jaw, nice lips, and well built.

His strong brows were perfectly manscaped into points on the ends, and he had a close, meticulously trimmed beard/mustache combo. Normally Vicki would melt into a puddle at the sight of such a specimen. But she regarded him skeptically.

"Buy you a drink?" he asked, standing confidently erect. He had the air of a man who could get any girl he wanted. The way he looked at her, like he'd start eating her at her head and wouldn't stop till he reached her toes, sent shards of excitement through her. Still, she didn't *need* to acquiesce. She wasn't the least bit horny, having been properly satisfied for the last couple of weeks.

"Thanks. Already have one."

"How about a dance, then?"

Vicki felt Amy's finger poke her rear end and dig in as if pointing her into the guy. Vicki downed a Kamikaze and said, "Sure." Then she downed her second shot and followed him.

He led her into the fray of undulating bodies bobbing to a song by The Weeknd. When he found a suitable place, he turned to her, raised his arms over his head, and swiveled his hips alluringly to the beat. Dark blue jeans hugged hip ridges that undulated like they were already making love to someone. A black vest with no shirt swished across his chest and abdomen, rippling with well-formed muscles. Not large, but he was definitely tight.

Vicki's eyes swept over him as she raised her own arms and swayed her hips, letting her low neckline dip further to expose more of her plump cleavage.

His eyes lingered on her breasts. "I'm Derek," he shouted over the music.

"Vicki."

"You're a great dancer, Vicki!"

"Thanks! You're not bad yourself." Having any kind of conversation over thumping-loud club music was impossible. Flirting was reduced to the shrieking of short sentences.

After they danced to a few songs, Vicki wanted to get a couple more shots before the special ended. "Drink?" she yelled.

Derek nodded, and they wiggled between dancers back to the bar. Amy was gone. Hopefully dancing with her own hottie. Vicki ordered two more Kamikazes.

"On me!" Derek called to the bartender, who nodded. Derek leaned against the bar, smiling. "So, what do you do during the daylight, Vicki?"

Masturbate. No, can't say that. "I work at a bank."

"Really? That must be cool."

She shrugged. "I guess. I'm in the offices on the upper floors. Accounts management."

"Nice!"

"What about you?"

"I'm an influencer on TikTok and Instagram."

"Oh? That pays?"

"It does when you have half a million followers on each."

"Wow. You must be very influential."

His chin raised. "I like to think so. I give men advice on how to be sexy. And I flex a little for the ladies." He twisted and curled his arm, bulging his biceps.

Vicki's eyes brightened. "Ooh. Very nice. I can see why you're so popular." She smiled, acting appropriately impressed. Honestly, he seemed like a bit of a chode, and despite all the penis she'd had lately, it'd be nice to have sex with a man attached to the member. Their shots arrived.

Two hours later, Derek pulled Vicki's dress over her head in his apartment. She'd gone to his place because, for some reason, she couldn't reconcile bringing another man home in front of her ... dildo. Yeah, this was definitely becoming unhealthy.

Derek flung his vest and pulled her close, stroking her sides with his fingertips and meeting her lips with an aggressive kiss. He quickly shed his pants and pushed her shoulders, so she fell back abruptly onto his bed. The dark blue comforter was heavily scented with cologne. The smell of a man. That was something she missed. And hands.

Derek grabbed her hips and yanked her to the edge of the bed, pulling off her panties and plunging his tongue into her opening.

Add 'tongue' to the list of things she missed.

Her head spun from all the shots she'd drunk. She wriggled blissfully under the suction of his mouth as he licked every fold and inched toward her clit. He reached it and sucked. She gasped and squealed. He continued flicking her nub with his tongue as her body responded with mounting vibrations of pleasure. He circled and teased until she clenched.

"Are you close?" he asked from between her legs.

"Yeah," she managed between gasps.

He quickly pulled a condom off his dresser, wrapped his erection, and stood at the end of the bed, pushing his cock into her.

"I'm gonna fuck you so hard." He held her calves up like he was about to make a wish, pulling her legs apart and plunging deeply into her.

Vicki shrieked as he rammed her.

"That's right. Scream for me." He moved a hand down to her clit and rubbed it gently but vigorously.

She exploded, gasping and screeching like a porn star. Her body lurched in a climax, but something felt off. Even with all the motion, and feeling her body being fondled and slammed, the cock inside her felt lifeless. It just shoved. Which was fine, but not as good as Goldwyn.

"Aw yeah. You got so wet when you came." He pulled out of her and flipped her onto her belly. "Get on your knees. I want to watch your ass bounce."

She complied, and he gripped her hips, thrusting into her rapidly, making a clapping sound.

"Fuck yeah. You're so fine." He sent a heavy palm across her ass cheeks with a smack.

Vicki yelped.

"You like it rough?" He spanked her again.

Not really. Just come already! Vicki braced against his vigorous thrusts. Finally, she heard it. The sound of his throat tightening as his sighs turned into squeaks. He was about to come. He gripped her haunches and furiously pounded her until he grunted like a bear scratching its ass on a pine tree.

When he finished, Derek pulled out and tossed the condom in his trash can. Vicki righted herself and sat up, scooting to lean against the headboard. He strutted across the bedroom. She watched his fine physique. He bent down to a mini fridge and grabbed two bottles of water from it. He sat next to her on the bed, and reached his hand to her head, drawing her in for a kiss. Then he handed her a bottle of water.

"Hydration is important. Water is life."

She eyed him. "Uh-huh."

He leaned against his headboard, drinking half his water in one long swig from the bottle. "Glad I met you tonight," he said. "You seem really cool."

She smiled. "Thank you."

"Can I talk about you on my next vee-log?"

"Umm ... I'd rather you didn't. Or, at least, don't mention my name. Or where you met me."

"Can do. I like to talk about my success stories. Oh, God! That was totally a rudeness! I didn't mean to make you sound like a conquest." He caressed her leg. "I'd actually really like to see you again. Can I take you to dinner or something sometime?"

Vicki let herself relax a little. Going home with a guy she met at a club was always a risky thing. Hit or miss. But she liked adventures, so she tried to have them whenever she could. Even if it was just a fuck. "I'd like that, Derek."

"Ohh, I like how you say my name. Kinda linger on the 'k' on the end. Sexy."

Her cheeks flushed.

"Is it cool if I go to sleep now? Got a lot of recording to do tomorrow, and I'm kinda drunk, so I know I'll be hungover. Def a kung pao chicken day tomorrow. You can crash here if you want to."

She huffed a giggle from her nose. "I appreciate that, but I think I'm gonna bounce. Let's get together next week or something, okay?"

"Yeah." He pivoted to her, brushed her cheek with a hand, and kissed her slowly. "Definitely."

Chapter Four

The Story

Vicki entered her townhouse and flicked on a light. Goldwyn lay on the coffee table, pointed at the door, as if he'd been waiting for her.

"Oh no. Did I leave you in the dark? Poor penis." She giggled. Still a bit drunk, and a little high from being with a man. She yanked off her platform heels, nearly falling over as she did so. Catching herself on the handrail to the stairs with a laugh, she said, "Amy invited me out. So, we went to this club. It was really fun." She decided not to mention Derek.

Vicki walked to the coffee table with a slight swagger in her step. She patted Goldwyn on his mushroom head. "Whoo! I'm a little swervy. I'm gonna go to bed." She turned and stumbled up her stairs.

Vicki stretched in the softness of her bed. In that space of waking, but not wanting to open her eyes yet, she rolled over and snuggled deeper into her pillow. The distinct feeling of being watched crept over her. She opened her eyes. An object nestled on the pillow next to her came into focus: the golden dildo, Goldwyn. Its helmet pointed at her and seemed to eye her with the hole in the tip.

She froze and took a sharp inhale. Slowly, fluidly, she backed away. She felt for the edge of the bed and reached for the floor with one foot while squirming backwards. Her body suddenly slipped over the mattress and she landed on the floor with a "Wahh!"

Gathering herself frantically, she hopped to her feet and looked at the dildo. It was hard. "You gotta be fucking kidding me," she muttered. "How the hell did you get there?"

It didn't move, but she almost expected it to.

"And why are you hard? You don't expect me to have morning sex with you, do you?" She cringed at her own words. "Why the fuck am I talking to my vibrator? What am I saying? I've been talking to it for two weeks!" She marched to the other side of the bed and picked it up. It began to flop.

"Oh, for the love of God! Do not sulk! Jesus Christ, what am I doing?" She went to her bureau and dropped Goldwyn into her underwear drawer. "I must be going crazy," she muttered herself as she slipped on a giant T-shirt and pulled on some panties. "I wasn't *that* drunk last night, but I must have brought it to bed with me."

She left her bedroom and went downstairs to her kitchen. "Why on earth would I do that? I mean, sure, I've had some of the best sex I've ever had with—" She jerked to a stop in the middle of her kitchen. "Can it even be considered sex?" she wondered. Vicki shook her head, trying to rid herself of the utter strangeness of the situation, as she reached for a coffee pod and plunked it into the coffeemaker.

Grabbing a mug from her cupboard, she continued talking to herself. "No. I *know* I didn't bring it to bed with me. Who sleeps with their dildo?" She shoved the mug under the spout of the coffee machine, punched the button, and waited impatiently for liquid gold to fill her cup.

"Especially after sleeping with an actual guy. No, I left it on the coffee table in the living room." She watched her mug fill. "Did I sleep walk?"

After flavoring her coffee with a caramel creamer, she settled in front of her laptop on the buffet counter. Greasy pizza cured everything. And that was exactly what she needed. She'd slept late, and it was already noon. Sipping her coffee, she pulled up a nearby pizza restaurant and placed an order for a thin crust with everything.

Vicki spent the day with Netflix again, munching pizza and relaxing. As the sun was going down, she heard a thud from upstairs. Pausing her show, she cocked her head to the side, listening hard to the silence. A moment later, she heard another thud. That one was quieter than the first. Her eyes flew to the stairs and she instinctively froze.

Maybe I left a window open? Unwilling to leave her perch to investigate, and refusing to be paranoid, she made herself comfortable again and lifted the remote to continue the show. But before she pressed play, a series of thumps came from her staircase.

She balled up on the couch, holding her remote over her head like a weapon as she watched Goldwyn, her golden dildo, roll-bounce down the stairs.

Roll ... thump. Roll ... thump.

She blinked hard. "I am *not* seeing this."

Goldwyn reached the bottom of the staircase, pivoted, and then rolled half the distance to the couch. Vicki hitched her rear end up until she was sitting on the arm of her couch, clutching her knees against her chest. "What the actual FUCK?"

The dildo buzzed and stopped.

"This is NOT happening."

Buzz.

After a few tight breaths, she asked, "A-are you ... possessed?"

Two buzzes.

"Um, okay. So, once for yes, twice for no?" she asked.

Buzz.

Vicki's breaths were quick and shallow. "Okay. So, what are you?"

Goldwyn was silent.

"I'm sorry, that wasn't a yes or no question. Umm. Are you alive?"

Buzz.

"Jesus!"

Buzz.

"Oh, God, are you a Christian?"

Goldwyn buzzed several times.

"Are you laughing?"

Buzz.

"Shit, this is weird."

Buzz.

Vicki released her legs to sit in a more relaxed position, but remained on the arm of her couch.

"So, okay. I have an alive dildo in my house. Totally normal."

Buzz, buzz.

"No? No to what? You're not alive?"

Buzz, buzz.

"Double negative. You are alive."

Buzz.

She searched her brain for how to ask pieces of her previous sentence with yes or no questions. "Are you a dildo?"

Buzz, buzz.

"Oh, my God!" Her mind whirled. "Are you a penis?"

Buzz.

"A real one?"

Buzz.

"Oh, God. Oh, my hell! Please tell me I haven't been masturbating with a disembodied real peen. Oh, ew!"

Buzz, buzz.

"You're not disembodied?"

Buzz, buzz.

Vicki was flummoxed. What else could a dick with no body be? "Is there more of you?"

Buzz.

She blinked. "Like—there's more of you?"

Buzz.

"Are you a man?"

Buzz.

"But not a ghost."

Buzz, buzz.

"Huh. I have no fucking idea how to work this out. I can't ask what happened to you. Or where the rest of you is." Then she remembered. "The witch lady!"

Buzzzzzzzzz.

"Ohhh. Are you like cursed or something?"

Buzz.

Vicki shifted. "I want to say that makes sense, but it doesn't. There's no such thing as magic and witchcraft, or curses."

Nothing.

"Goldwyn, is magic real?"

Buzz.

She drew her hand along her face in disbelief. "Okay, I gotta know: can you see me?"

Buzz.

She smiled. "Do you like me?"

Buzz, buzz, buzz, buzz.

"Okay, okay." She giggled, blushing. The complete insanity of this predicament hit her again. It was one thing to talk to a dildo. It was another when it talked back. Was this real? Or was she hangover-talking to a vibrator? She asked, "Do you have a name?"

Buzz.

Her smile deepened. Realizing that she was talking to a man was almost comforting in a way. Even if he was somehow trapped in his own dick. At least her vibrator wasn't possessed by a demon or something.

"Well, trying to guess what your name is will be problematic. Wait! I have an idea." She hopped off the couch and ran to the kitchen, where she kept a notepad for her grocery list. She returned to the living room with the pad and a pen. "I'm going to write the alphabet down. You buzz once when I hit the letters for your name, okay?"

Buzz.

She went through the letters until Goldwyn buzzed three times, signaling he was done.

"Arthur?"

Buzz.

"Want to go for your last name?"

Buzz.

She went through the alphabet again. "Arthur Johnson," she announced when they'd finished.

Buzz.

Vicki looked at the golden phallus laying on her carpet. "Isn't Johnson another term for a ..." She giggled, then her heart filled with sorrow. She regarded the sad-looking penis, laying limply on the floor. "You poor thing. You're just a piece of a man, aren't you?"

After a pause, it buzzed.

"Jesus. I'm so sorry, Arthur." Her heart sank. "I guess I should introduce myself formally. I'm Vicki. Victoria Terry."

Buzz.

"Can I ask how old you are?"

Buzz.

"Stop me when I hit the first digit. One."

Nothing.

163

"Two."

Buzz.

"Okay, second digit. One, Two, Three ..."

Arthur buzzed at four.

"You're only twenty-four?"

Buzz.

"Ghastly. I'm twenty-seven. Guess you're fucking an older woman!"

A series of buzzes, indicating his laughter, erupted from him.

"Okay, next I want to know when this happened to you." Vicki asked questions with yes or no answers, the alphabet, and numbers until she learned Arthur was born in 1922 and had been transformed in 1946. The woman who had transformed him was named Patricia. She was one-hundred years old when she passed away.

"Wow. You're not really twenty-four. You're more like one-hundred-and-two!

Buzz.

"Arthur, do you know any way we can free you?"

Buzz, buzz.

"Damn." By this time, Vicki was sitting on the floor in front of the golden penis. She stroked him affectionately in a soothing motion. "I'm so sorry this happened to you."

The phallus vibrated in a soft rhythm, as if it was purring. "I can do some research. Maybe I can find a way to free you." She picked him up and kissed his mushroom head. Arthur stiffened slightly.

"No. No, Arthur. I think we should just cuddle tonight."

Chapter Five

The Next Surprise

V icki sat at her laptop, pouring over searches on how to break curses. All of it was theoretical, and none of it serious. Much of the lore indicated that if the person who did the cursing died, then the curse would be broken. But that certainly wasn't the case for Arthur.

The sun dipped, and her eyes drooped in fatigue. Arthur rolled up to her.

"I don't think I can stare at this computer anymore. I'm sorry, but I haven't found anything that's very helpful. Everything says that after she died, you should have been freed." She bent down from her chair and patted the shiny cock. "I'm gonna take a shower. Then, let's watch a movie, okay?

Buzz.

Vicki showered, and when she returned to her living room, Arthur was waiting on the floor by the couch. She picked him up and laid him in her lap like a kitten as she scrolled through Netflix movie thumbnails.

"Now that I know you really are a man in there, I don't feel as weird talking to you. Even though this whole thing is weird." She stroked his shaft absently as she scrolled. Arthur released a series of happy vibrations as though he was purring. When she found something acceptable on Netflix, she clicked on it and reclined against the arm of her couch. She brought Arthur up onto her chest and smooched his tip.

"Comfy?" she asked.

Buzz.

"Can you see the TV?"

Buzz.

"Good."

The show she'd selected was a spicy series about a love triangle. The sex scenes were luscious and explicit. She looked at Arthur nestled between her breasts. "How do you think they film those? I mean, it looks like they're actually doing it. Where does the guy put his dick if it's not in her? Gotta be taped to his leg or something, cuz damn."

Arthur rumbled buzzes of laughter.

The characters in the show were fit. Vicki's breath deepened and her skin heated as she watched the male lead's muscular ass clench as he appeared to thrust into the female lead. Arthur's tip caressed the corner of her mouth. Absently, she kissed it.

He pressed against her lips and pushed into her mouth a little. She opened her lips and licked his crown. Her tongue traced circles around Arthur's tip and fondled the little hole in the center. Arthur trembled.

Opening wider, Vicki wrapped her mouth around his tip and sucked. Gently, she took his shaft and held it as her suction brought him deeper into her mouth. She sucked, glided her tongue under his shaft, and squeezed her grip around him. Arthur swelled and lengthened.

She pulled him from her mouth to speak. "Arthur, I have to know; are you feeling pleasure?"

Buzz.

"Do you like having sex with me?"

Buzz, buzz, buzz, buzz.

She giggled. "Do you want me now?"

Buzz, buzz, buzz, buzz.

"Can you do it all on your own?"

Arthur answered by rolling down her chest and vibrating on one of her nipples. "Hold on a sec, my clothes are in the way." Vicki sat up, placed Arthur on the couch, and pulled off her shirt and panties. She laid back on the cushions, and returned him to her naked breasts.

He vibrated on a nipple, then rolled to vibrate gently on the tip of her other breast. She sighed. He rolled down her belly heading for her crotch. She scooted her hips so she could lay back and spread her thighs to receive what he wanted to give.

The golden dildo rolled to her hot cleft. She closed her eyes. He buzzed against her thigh and rolled slowly inward, sending his magical vibrations through her body. Roll by tantalizing roll, he closed in until he was on her clit. She moaned. The vibrating tip moved down and rolled back and forth until he'd parted her labia and was pressing against her opening, making her as wet as a rainy day. The spongy mushroom helmet pushed teasingly into her slit and rotated.

"God, that feels so good, Arthur." She groaned.

He continued rotating, boring into her with his plump cap, and vibrated quickly against a sensitive spot right inside her opening.

"Ahh ... oohhh" she cooed. "So good."

His tip pulled hot moisture from her, lubricating himself, and then rose until he pressed against her clit.

"God, Arthur, yes. Right there." She stretched and grasped for the edges of her couch, bracing for the wonderful warmth and delicious ecstasy he spread through her with every movement.

The penis glided downward and slowly penetrated her.

"Yesss ..."

He thrust deeply into her. As her golden vibrator slowly and deliberately fucked her, Vicki began feeling a weight upon her. It was like she was being held down by something. The sensation of a hand stroking her breast surprised her and her eyes flew open.

The ghostly apparition of a man hovered over her. His pale blue eyes stared affectionately. His touch centered on her nipple, and pinched gently.

"Arthur?"

He smiled and bent his head close to her. She felt warm, real lips press against hers. Arms embraced her and a tongue slid between her lips to glide against her own. She closed her eyes again, kissing him deeply.

Hard hips met the inner softness of her thighs and lunged, pushing his vibrating cock deeply in eliciting quick, sharp sighs from her. Vicki didn't understand it, but there was a man on her and inside her. Not a dildo. She brought her own arms around the apparition, testing his solidity. She felt hot, soft skin and a strong, muscular frame.

He was now as solid and real as she was.

"Arthur ..."

He kissed her again and then stared at her. He brought a hand up and caressed her face. Gently, he thrust his cock, and she groaned. He slowly rocked her with a tender, fascinated smile on his mouth. She ran her hands along his muscular torso.

"Can you speak?"

"I don't know." The sound surprised him as much as it did her, and his face exploded with mirth. "Well, I'll be! Can you hear me, Vicki?"

"Yes! I can hear you." She cupped his face with her hands. His blond hair was cut closely around his head except for a mass of curls on the top. "I can see you! Oh, God, and I can feel you."

He thrust playfully hard into her, making her gasp.

"I've been doing this to you the whole time. Only you couldn't see me," he said.

"How is this possible?" she asked breathily.

His thrusting cock rattled her sanity. She found it hard to talk through the pleasure, much less keep her senses now that his whole body pushed against her.

"I don't really know. Maybe it's because you've been treating me like a person. All that attention and energy must have built up—Ungh," he grunted with pleasure, "giving me strength so I can appear." His lips pressed to hers. "I've wanted to tell you how beautiful you are."

"You have?" her eyes nearly crossed.

His hips ground into her thighs as his abdomen dragged against her clit. "I've wanted to tell you that you make me so happy."

"You have?"

He swooped his mouth down to kiss her again.

"I've longed to feel these lips." He pressed a demanding suction to her mouth, sending his tongue in deeply and capturing the last of her sanity.

Vicki joined his movements with her hips, returning his grind and wrapping her legs around him. She clutched and scooped against him. His fantastic cock worked its magic inside her until warm flutters began to erupt in her core.

"Arthur ..." She writhed against his body, reveling in the friction.

"Yes, Vicki."

"You're gonna make me come."

"No. Not yet."

"I can stop it." The explosion started, and she moaned with every thrust until she cried out.

"God, Arthur! Yes!" She squeezed her eyes shut. His arms scooped around her, his hands gripping her shoulders as his movements quickened. He drove into her until she was screaming at the top of her lungs. He gasped and grunted with her.

"Victoria ..." he whispered in her ear. And then he was gone.

Chapter Six

The Rules

V icki lay panting, recovering from an orgasm that had just rocked her bones. The man who was kissing and holding her vanished. She looked at her belly to see the golden dildo protruding from her cunt.

Her head flopped back. "What is happening?" she wailed to the empty room and pulled the vibrator from her body. The golden dick was becoming limp. "Arthur?"

Buzz.

"Oh, thank God. I thought maybe I was hallucinating."

Buzz, buzz.

Vicki placed him on her chest and petted him. "I think—" she took some breaths, still recovering. "I think you can only materialize when you're in use. If ya know what I mean."

Buzz.

"You disappeared as soon as I came. As soon as you fulfilled your purpose, so to speak." She heaved a sigh. "Now that we can talk. We'll have to make love again so I can learn more."

Buzzzzzzz

She giggled. "You like that, do you?"

The phallus buzzed several times.

Vicki cackled. When her breaths normalized, she said, "You're very handsome, you know." She stroked the shaft with her fingertips. "And you're a great kisser."

He responded with several short buzzes. He seemed happy, and she contentedly enjoyed the afterglow. She yawned and stretched.

"I'm tired. I need to wash you. Then let's go to bed."

Buzz.

When she carried him to her room, she laid him upon the pillow next to hers and cuddled into the blankets. She fell asleep with her hand on him.

Vicki woke to the sensation of a gentle vibrating nudge against her crotch. She moaned, unwilling to wake completely, but rolled onto her back. Arthur was hard and followed her movements to push against her clit. The hot tingles he inspired spread through her and she widened her legs. He slid down and inside her. After a few thrusts, the beautiful man from the night before materialized. Vicki opened her eyes to see his sparkling eyes and face solidify.

"Good morning, gorgeous," he said, with a gentle push of his hips.

She smiled. "Morning."

"I loved sleeping next to you last night."

"You sleep?"

"Yeah. It's how I charge. You probably noticed I don't have any batteries."

She giggled. "That's something I had a question about. There weren't dildos like you, in the forties."

Arthur caressed her breasts as he spoke. "When Patricia cursed me, she was very specific about what she wanted."

"Why did she curse you, Arthur?"

His movements ceased, and he leaned on his forearms. "Golly, I— It's kind of embarrassing."

Vicki caressed his face and kissed him softly. "Tell me."

"She was jealous."

"Ohh. That can be tricky."

"I was quite the Casanova, see."

"How am I not surprised?"

His grin spread and he gave her a playful thrust. "I was popular at the dance halls. I'd get a little sauced, cut a rug, find a beautiful dame, and take her home. Patricia had her eye on me for a while. But I wasn't too keen on her. Great pegs, but that was it. Not a looker. I turned her down all the time. Guess she didn't take kindly to that. Besides, there was this one gal I was getting a little sweet on. She gave me thoughts about settling down. I was thinking of letting her make an honest man outta me. Until Patricia blew it all up."

"Oh, Arthur, I'm so sorry."

His head lowered dourly. Golden curls flopped over his brows. He began to fade.

"No! Arthur, stay with me." Vicki pumped her hips.

His arms strengthened around her and he thrust until he solidified. He kissed her deeply and ground long, rhythmic thrusts into her. Before she knew it, she was moaning and coming, and he vanished.

"Dammit! We could keep talking if the sex wasn't so good. She felt him vibro-laugh inside her. She pulled him out. "We'll pick this up later. I need to get ready for work." She got out of bed, and taking Arthur with her, went to the kitchen for coffee. She washed him in the sink while her caffeine brewed.

"Do you like coffee?"

Buzz.

"God, it must be frustrating being in the state you're in. I can't even imagine the boredom."

Buzz.

Once her coffee was ready, she carried it and Arthur to her laptop. Perching on a stool at the buffet counter, she opened and typed a search for his name. Old newspaper articles populated the screen.

"Oh, my God. Look at this! She pointed his tip at the laptop so he could see. 'Local man, Arthur Johnson, goes missing.'" She read out loud. "Arthur Johnson, twenty-four, has been missing since Saturday. He was last seen at the Hopper Room. Witness, Gayle Clemens, said the two spent the night dancing, and she didn't observe any signs of distress in Johnson. Clemens said the pair even made plans for the following Saturday night. She had no reason to think he'd leave town.

"This could be a case of foul play. Johnson's parents have reported no sign of their son and are desperate for news. Any information about Johnson should be directed to the local police department." Vicki's sad eyes turned to the wilted golden penis laying sullenly on the counter. "Gayle. That was the girl?"

There was a hesitant, soft buzz.

"Jeez. How completely tragic. God, I'm so sorry, sweetheart. Your girl, your family, your friends. You lost everybody you knew."

Arthur remained silent.

"And I guess none of them would be alive now to even tell that you've been found."

Arthur rolled off the buffet counter, fell with a thud to the floor, and rolled away.

Vicki hopped up. "Shit. I'm sorry, Arthur!" She trotted over to him as he rolled to the couch. "That was very insensitive of me. Look, I need to go to work. Let's talk more tonight."

Buzz.

That night, she placed him on the couch. "Are you feeling better?"

Buzz.

"Better enough to tell me the rest of your story?"

Buzz.

Vicki pulled off her clothes and set the golden penis end up on a couch cushion. First, she teased the tip with her lips and tongue. He responded by straightening and engorging. She held onto the shaft, sucking vigorously until she heard a sigh.

"God, that feels so good," he said. Arthur had formed and was sitting on the couch.

She continued jacking him, so he'd stay solid. "Look at this! You don't have to be inside me to be real."

175

"Just don't stop touching my dick."

She leaned over and grabbed a tube of lotion from the coffee table, made herself comfortable on her knees in front of him, and added lotion to her strokes.

"Tell me more about what happened."

"Well, one night, I was heading back to my place, and I got a knock on the head." He gestured at his curly crown. "Patricia had hired some thug to drag me to her place. I woke up naked and tied to her kitchen chair."

"Oh, my God! She must have been really desperate."

"She was whack-job, that's what. Loose in the head. She told me she'd seen me and Gayle getting close and she didn't like that."

"Sheesh. What a bitch."

He nodded. "Patricia wasn't any kind of special. She wasn't even a real witch. She paid some black-magic woman for the spell."

"Did she perform it herself?"

He shook his head. "No. Some voodoo broad did it."

"Arthur! That's why you haven't transformed! She must still be alive!"

"No. No chance, doll. That lady's long dead. She was old when she performed the spell."

"My hand's getting tired." Vicki released him and stood to quickly straddle him before he faded away. She slid onto his erection. He must be almost eight inches long. A fact made clear as she sat, pushing him so deep, she almost couldn't take it. "Goddamn, you've got a huge cock."

He smirked. "I'll never get used to how you gals talk these days. Guys are vulgar. But I've never heard a woman swear so much."

"You're gonna have to get used to it. Especially if you keep fucking me so good."

Arthur made a growling sound. He grabbed the hair, pulled her head back, and bit the tender flesh of her neck, nibbling down to her clavicle. His other hand pushed her ass, gliding her along his girth.

"You have no idea how hard it is to wait here all day for you to come home. All I want is you. All I think about is fucking you ... all ... day ... long." He bit her neck again, keeping a firm grasp of her hair.

She groaned. "Yes. Fuck me, Arthur. Pull my hair harder!"

He yanked her dark locks, and she squealed.

"God, yes!" Vicki bounced vigorously on him, shrieking with delight.

"Fuck! Arthur, I think this conversation is over." She jerked and ground her clit as she screamed from an orgasm. After her shaking climax, he disappeared. She plummeted to the couch. The shaft of his penis protruded from her pussy. She pulled it out. "I'm never gonna get used to that."

Chapter Seven

The Choice

For the next week, Vicki and Arthur kept their routine. She'd tell him about her day, then they'd fuck and talk until she came and he disappeared. They created a wonderful little bubble of secret bliss. She hadn't even told Amy about it. But even in her newfound happiness, she wasn't any closer to discovering a solution to Arthur's predicament. Then, fucking started to turn into making love and it spooked her.

One morning as she showered for work, her mind spiraled with questions. The reality of their situation vexed her. After this much constant conversation and great sex with a normal guy, she'd be wondering if this relationship might be going somewhere significant. But where could this go? Nothing about this was regular, or normal, or rational.

As she shampooed her hair, she wondered how could she and Arthur have any kind of ordinary relationship? What was the endgame here? What was she supposed to do? Marry her dildo? That'd be an awkward ceremony—the bride jacking the groom while they said their vows and exchanged rings. It was ridiculous.

Vicki lathered body wash along her skin. What about when she grew old? She envisioned herself as an old woman having yes/no conversation with a golden buzzing schlong. She shook her head at the absurdity of it and rinsed the soap off. She remained a moment under the shower head, as if the running water could soothe her brain.

Why am I thinking about this? Marriage? Old age? She leaned against the tile in her shower. *Because I'm starting to have feelings for him, that's why. Maybe I should slow this down. Or end it.* But the thought of ending it didn't relieve her heavy heart. It made her feel worse.

Their conversations had steered from solving the mystery of breaking his curse to sharing their lives. They told stories about their childhoods and life experiences. They were bonding. Maybe it was time to put some space between herself and Arthur. Whatever feelings were developing needed to be tempered. This had to stay casual.

Another wrinkle appeared when she started getting texts from Derek. He'd actually meant it when he said he wanted to see her again. The first text came on a Tuesday

> **Derek:** You've been on my mind. I'd really like to see you again. Dinner Friday? It'd be nice to have a good conversation with a beautiful woman.

"Huh. That's actually a nice text," Vicki said out loud as she ate her lunch in the break room. He struck her as more of a dick-pic man.

Lina overheard. "Something special?" she asked, smiling.

Vicki's eyes flicked from her phone to Lina's face. "Um, yeah. This guy I met wants to take me out."

"That's nice! What's his name?"

"Derek. He says he's some kind of social media influencer."

"Derek?" Lina's eyes bulged. "Derek 'Double D' Drake?"

Vicki blinked. "I have no idea."

Lina shoved her phone in Vicki's face. "Is this him?"

The profile of Derek Drake displayed on the screen. Long brown locks and perfectly sculpted facial hair.

"Yep. That's him."

"No way! No way you're dating Double D!"

"Uhh, yeah. Well, kind of. He wants to take me out Friday. I haven't responded yet."

Lina gave a groan like she was going to dissolve with envy right into the floor. Settling back into her chair, she said, "Oh, my God, you *have* to go! Then I can live vicariously through you. Just tell me everything, okay?"

Vicki cringed internally. "Sure will." She bit into her sandwich. Realizing that Derek was actually mildly famous sent a little thrill through her. She opened Instagram on her phone and found his profile. She clicked on one of his videos. He was wearing an open dress shirt, showing off his hard chest, much like he did in the club.

"Okay, gentlemen. When in pursuit of your vixen, you must begin gently. Use your nicest vocabulary at first, okay? Be that sweet, sweet honey that they just can't resist. Only after some time should you ramp up the fuck-talk, okay?

"I hear you asking me, Derek, when is the right time to ramp up the fuck-talk? I'm glad you asked that. Curiosity is *good!* It shows critical thinking, and that's a skill you'll need with your vixen for the long game. Okay? So, I'd say the best time to start the fuck-talk is during and or after the first time you sex your vixen. During sex, women are more open and suggestible. Showing your dominance while you sex her is a sure way to get you another date, *and* will open that door to the fuck-talk."

"Fuck-talk?" Vicki snorted and rolled her eyes. *So far, he seems to follow his own advice. He's definitely got douche tendencies, but he's also pretty funny.* She texted him back.

> **Vicki:** I'm looking forward to seeing you again too. Friday sounds good.

> **Derek:** Excellent! I can't wait to look into those baby browns again.

Vicki's tummy shimmied.

> **Vicki:** One of my coworkers just had a meltdown when I told her I was having dinner with you.

> **Derek:** Aw that's sweet! I love my fans! They're the best! Tell her I said hi!

"Hey, Lina! Derek says to tell you hi."

"What?" Lina shrieked. "Oh, my God!"

On Thursday, Derek's text was a little more aggressive. He must have been testing Vicki's receptiveness to his so-called fuck-talk.

Derek: Thinking about your beautiful, perfect ass all day. It's been torture.

Vicki: Stop thinking about it then! LOL.

Derek: No way! LOL!

As the week went on, the situation with Arthur bothered Vicki more and more. She couldn't find any way to help him, and she stopped having sex with him because she needed to avoid getting emotionally attached to her dildo-man. *Manbrator? Vibroman?*

Sure, Arther was a nice guy. He was fun, sweet, great to talk to, handsome, and fantastic in the sack. But her mind always circled back to how impossible being with him long term would be.

The temptation Derek offered, with no curses attached, wore her down. A real flesh and bone man wanted her, and she couldn't ignore that. She had to give her life a chance. Especially since there was no obvious solution to Arthur's situation.

Then she wondered how she could have any normal relationship when her vibrator turned into Arthur every time she used him? That was too close to cheating in her book. Especially since it—he—actually *was* a real man.

She'd have to part with Arthur if she wanted to have a relationship with someone else. But the thought of that only upset her further.

Derek's text on Friday was even more provocative.

Derek: Tonight's the night! Got a sweet little Greek restaurant picked out. Then I want to take you home and make you scream again.

Vicki: I love Greek food. And I bet you say that to all your success stories.

Derek: LOL Nope. Just you Vicki. BTW, do you want it fast and rough, or slow and soft tonight?

Vicki's belly somersaulted and her clit gave her a little throb. *Holy shit! I can't believe it! He's following his own steps, and it's actually working on me. I legit can't wait to see him.*

Vicki: Let's start slow and end rough.

Derek: That sounds perfect.

She most looked forward to his tongue on her cunt. And having a normal conversation without being attached at the crotch would be nice.

When she got home that night, Arthur was on the coffee table waiting for her. She'd left the TV on for him. Something she started doing once she realized he was sentient.

"Hey Arthur. How was your day? Mine was more of the same. So glad it's Friday." She kicked off her shoes and hung her purse. "Listen, Amy invited me out tonight. I think I'm gonna go."

Buzz, buzz.

"Listen, I know I haven't used you in a few days. I told you I needed a small break. I like having a lot of sex, but sometimes, I just need some time off."

Buzzzzz, buzz, buzz, buzzzzz.

"Arthur, please don't throw a fit. This situation is so bizarre. I know you can only be yourself and talk when we're screwing, and I know that's frustrating, but I have a life too. I can't stay home and fuck all the time."

He sat silently. It tugged her heart, but what kind of life could she have with a man trapped in his own dick?

Her head hung regretfully. "I'm gonna get ready to go. We're having dinner first." She hopped up her stairs. She didn't like lying to him, but she couldn't go on like they were in a regular relationship.

Vicki met Derek at the Greek restaurant and they spent dinner chatting about fitness and flirting. It was mundane. Wonderfully mundane and normal. Vicki couldn't believe that, even though she was a little bored with the conversation, she was in public with a normal guy talking about boring things, and the ordinary nature of it actually thrilled her.

Even so, her mind kept drifting to Arthur. She thought of his lovely light blue eyes and their hint of sadness. He had an intensity underlying his playful demeanor that she adored.

By the time dinner was over, she felt guilty about being out with Derek. He paid the bill, and she left the tip.

He stood and put his arm around her, walking her to the parking lot. When they got to her car, Derek turned, rested a curved finger under her jaw, raised her chin, and tenderly stroked his thumb along her lips. His eyes held hers until their lips touched.

He leaned his forehead against hers. "I'm so ready to be inside you again," he said.

Vicki took his hands. "Derek, I don't think I can go home with you tonight."

"What? Why not?"

Yeah, why not? "Umm ... Because I'm kinda dating another guy too. It feels weird to be sleeping with both of you. I need to cut it off with him first."

He stood up straight. "Oh, I see. I got competition. Got another cock to fight."

She pinched her eyebrows in confusion.

"You know. Like a rooster. A cock fight?" He chortled. "Sorta like a double entendre. Get it?" He chuckled again.

It surprised her that Derek even knew what an entendre was. She gave a polite giggle through her nose. "Yeah. I guess so."

"Okay, but don't leave without this." He pressed his lips into hers aggressively. His tongue parted her lips in a tonsil-tickling kiss. Derek caressed her arms, then smoothed around her back, holding her sturdily in his embrace.

She responded, holding him and sweeping her tongue along his as her cunt moistened. *God, he really is good. But I have to figure out what I'm doing with Arthur first.* When he released her, she swayed on her feet a little.

"You keep that close," he whispered.

"I will." Vicki got into her car before she let him bend her over in the parking lot. It had been a few of days, after all, and she was getting horny. Ironically, she'd abstained from Arthur so she wouldn't feel slutty about sleeping with Derek. And now she was turning Derek down so she could stay with Arthur.

"Man, I really need to get my head straight," she said to herself as she drove.

When she got home, Arthur was still laying on the coffee table watching TV. He pivoted towards her when she walked through the front door.

"I'm so sorry Arthur!" she blurted, dropping to her knees and petting his golden shaft. "I lied to you. I went on a date."

The phallus rumbled but didn't exactly buzz. She interpreted that as anger.

Her voice turned sorrowful. "Don't be mad. It was just dinner. I won't lie to you again. I did consider going to go home with him, but it felt wrong. I guess I realized that you're really special to me." She planted a little kiss on his helmet. "I think I'm having some feelings and I'm not sure what to do about them. But they scared me, and that's why I ..." She sighed. "Arthur, be honest with me. Are you having feelings for me too?"

There was a brief pause, then he buzzed once.

Vicki's heart warmed happily. "I want to help you. I don't want to give up on-on whatever this is. I'm not sure what kind of future we could have. And we may need to reconcile that at some point. But for now—"

A knock sounded on the door.

"Who on earth could that be?" Vicki pushed up and looked through the peephole in the door. It was Derek. "Holy shit." She whirled to Arthur. "It's him," she whispered. "Don't move." She opened the door. "Derek! What are you doing here?"

He stepped in and closed the door behind him. "I followed you. Thought it would be romantic." He pulled her into his arms and kissed her. "I wanted to show you I mean business," he said huskily. "Maybe convince you to let me into that hot sweetness between your thighs again."

Arthur rattled on the coffee table.

Derek and Vicki both looked to see the gold penis vibrating furiously. He was fully erect and shook with unmistakable agitation.

A wide grin split Derek's face. "Oh wow! Is that my competition?" He took a couple confident steps towards the coffee table.

Eyes bulging, Vicki clutched her mouth with both hands.

Derek pivoted back to her. "Were you about to use it? Heh! Good thing I showed up." He bent down to examine it.

Arthur stilled.

"Man, look at this thing. It's so—OW!"

Arthur reared up and jutted his mushroom tip into Derek's eye. Derek stumbled back, "What the hell?"

"Oh, my God. Arthur, no!" Vicki shouted.

"Arthur?" Derek looked completely confused.

The gilded penis levitated off the table and met Derek at face level.

Derek eyes popped wildly. "What the fuck is going on here?"

"Arthur, don't," Vicki pleaded.

Arthur ignored her and swung at Derek's head, thwapping him back and forth across the face several times until Derek batted it down.

"What the *fuck*," he yelled, "is that thing?"

The golden cock floated and soared like a javelin straight at Derek, who jumped backwards until his back was against the door. The helmet tip of the dildo hovered menacingly a few inches from Derek's eye.

"I'm—I'm, uh, gonna leave, now. Okay? Okay dick? N-nice dick. Please don't poke my eye again."

Vicki'd had enough. She snatched Arthur from the air and gripped him firmly. "Okay, you've made your point. Now, calm down."

"Shit!" Derek flung open the door and ran into the night.

Vicki shouted out the front door. "Hey Double D! Can you *not* put this on your vee-log?"

Chapter Eight

The Admission

V icki closed her front door. She held Arthur at eye-level. "What was that?"

He buzzed.

She stomped into her living room. "I know we need to talk. But after that display, I'm not sure I want to fuck you right now!"

He buzzed again.

Fine. I'll get you hard, but don't expect sex. I'm far too annoyed." She set the phallus on her couch and stroked it. Its tip raised and pointed to her lips.

"Oh, you want kisses? I'm not sure you deserve kisses right now." He vibed pleadingly.

"Ugh." She kissed the tip and urgently sucked over the mushroom crown. She wasn't interested in pleasing him; just wanted him to form so he could explain himself.

Vicki sucked down along the shaft and she felt him harden and swell. Adding strokes to her suction, she finally heard a sigh. Hands grabbed her arms and pulled her up as he stood and brought her in for an impassioned kiss. His arms, strong and demanding, held her to him as his tongue slid into her mouth to play with hers. Vicki's knees weakened, and she returned his embrace.

He pulled from her lips and stroked her hair, staring yearningly into her eyes. "I'm sorry, Victoria. I wasn't about to let that fat-head man-handle you in front of me. It was too much." He desperately kissed her again. "Forgive me. I went into a jealous rage." He caressed her cheek. "I don't know how crazy I'd go if I lost you, and I don't want to find out."

The heated touch of his lips and strong sweeps from his tongue disintegrated her.

"Arthur! You're still solid and we aren't—"

"Would you look at that!" he wondered. "I am pretty hard, though. And I must be pleasing ya somehow." His wide grin displayed.

Vicki melted and ran her fingers through the curls on the top of his head. She let her touch glide down the back of his neck and shoulders. He was so finely made. Muscles bulging deliciously. Her hands landed on the small of his back and then gently made their way down his rear end. He flexed.

She giggled. "I gotta say, the look on his face when a dildo levitated in the air and then bitch slapped him was fucking hilarious."

Arthur laughed.

"It's dangerous though," she said, "exposing yourself like that."

"I know." He hung his head. "But it's like I said. I had to do somethin'. That creep was really trying to get at ya. I couldn't allow that. Not after what you told me when you came home." He started fading.

Vicki gently stroked his shaft until he solidified again.

"You really do care about me," he said in awe. "No foolin'?"

She smiled up at him. "No foolin'. I'm not sure how this is going to work. But I want to help you. If we don't work out after that, fine. But at least you'll have your life back."

"Why wouldn't we work out? You're about the best damned woman I've ever known."

She flung her head back with a joy-filled laugh.

He tenderly gripped her chin. "I mean it, Victoria. I may have spent the last several decades in some old hag's hog-eyed-flap-cave, but I know a good woman when I see one. And you're quality."

Vicki nearly collapsed laughing. "Hog-eyed-flap-cave?"

"What? Yeah. Her mole catcher. Her whisker biscuit. God, she was gross."

Vicki fell against him, howling with giggles, desperately trying to keep stroking him, but ended up giving him a series of jarring yanks until he faded again.

"Victoria! Take me upstairs," he said before he vanished and flopped onto the couch.

She fell onto the cushions, convulsing until her giggle fit subsided. She stood and picked his dick up. He was buzzing with laughter.

Vicki went to her bedroom and turned on a light. She lay Arthur's cock on the bed. "Do you want me to undress?"

Buzz.

"Okay. Prepare yourself, sailor."

Buzzzzzz.

She began slowly taking off her clothes. One button at a time, she strip-teased, flinging each item onto the floor as she pulled them off. The gold penis stiffened. When she pulled off her bra, she fondled her breasts and twisted the hardening tips.

The cock rumbled softly.

She slid her panties down, spread her legs, and fondled herself. She drew silky wetness from her cunt and fingered it up to her clitoris, sighing as she did so.

To her surprise, Arthur formed right there, without her even touching him. His knees casually hung over the bedside, and his hands were folded behind his head.

He said, "Hot damn, Victoria. That's about the sexiest thing I've ever seen."

"Oh my God, Arthur! You're here, and I'm not even touching you."

He raised up on his elbows. "I'm cocked up enough to fire at the Germans. Maybe that's it." He pushed up to stand in front of her. He grazed her skin with the gentlest touch, running his hands down her naked body. Stepping closer, he pressed his lips to hers.

Fire burned through her. Something about him made her ache. She'd never felt anything like it. She opened her mouth and kissed him deeply, fondling his tight hips and dragging her nails down the front of his pelvis to his thighs.

He shivered. She clasped his back as he took a few steps as though he was dancing with her. He turned her body and backed her against the bed. Settling onto the mattress, she scooted to its center. He crawled over, overwhelming her with his exploring mouth and hands.

He worked down her body pressing, hot kisses as he went. His teeth grazed her skin, and he nipped at her breasts and firm nipples. Taking a moment, he sucked and fondled the plump mounds of her chest, inspiring happy sighs from her. His lips continued their kissing trail down to her cleft. Vicki shivered in anticipation.

Arthur's hot tongue slid along the delicacies between her thighs. A flick nipped her clitoris, and she moaned. His mouth descended upon it, working the flesh with his tongue and lips. He slowly inserted two fingers inside her wet opening and deftly probed her pliant depths.

Vicki lunged her hips with every luxurious plunge of his fingers, and every exquisite suck from his mouth. The sensations were so bright, so vivid, she saw colors behind her closed eyelids.

"Don't make me come yet," she begged.

Arthur stopped, licked up her belly, pausing for another nibbling suck on her nipples. She caressed his torso, enjoying every rippled rise and fall of his muscular structure.

"You really are beautiful, Arthur."

A smile spread across his lips. "Thanks doll. That's a leftover from my time in the service."

It donned on her that he must have fought in World War II. Her eyes widened.

Reading her expression, he cut her off. "Don't ask, okay? I don't wanna talk about it right now. I just want to make love to you. Fucking you is the best. But I want to love you tonight." His hot exhale tickled her face.

Vicki smiled sweetly. "Can't remember the last time someone took the time to make love to me." She opened her legs and let him nestle into her.

"That's a real shame," he said. "A gal like you deserves the time it takes to savor her."

Warmth consumed her as his fingertips strode along the sensitive skin of her thighs. Aurthur's hand rounded her ass cheek, then pulled her leg up and drew his firm erection along her opening. She strengthened her embrace and kissed him deeply, drawing the firmness of his erection along her cunt until his tip sank in. He played with her. Dipping in until she clenched around him, then pulling out. After teasing her to a whimpering frenzy, he pushed in slowly. She broke their kiss so she could gasp his name.

"God, Arthur ..."

He recaptured her mouth and thrust with agonizing, leisurely plunges.

"Ya feel that?" he asked. "That's a connection, doll."

"It's wonderful," she breathed, raising her hips into him and following his movements.

Their hands glided over each other's skin as their bodies slid together in unison. Arthur dipped to suckle her nipples between kissing her and sighing heavily, drenching Victoria in an ocean of love and pleasure.

A deep tickle vibrated inside her. She pushed against him, and their breathing deepened. He churned into her.

"Arthur, you're gonna make me come."

"Victoria, I gotta say somethin'. I think I'm falling for ya."

She searched his baby blues. "Yeah?"

"Yeah."

"Ahh ... oohhh," she gasped. "Me too." Tremors consumed her and her squeals grew louder as every wave of her orgasm strengthened until she screamed. He thrust harder, keeping pace with her spasming body until he grunted and gasped with her. They clung to each other, coming hard. Vicki didn't want it to end.

She didn't want him to disappear. They slowed, and he kissed her until he evaporated.

"Ah, dammit! I hate that part!" She slammed the bed with her fists. "Just once I want to cuddle with you after." She brought her hands up to her face, covering her eyes.

Buzz.

She reached down and pulled him out of her. Grieving the sudden absence of his body, she rolled over curling inwards, cradling her treasured phallus.

Chapter Nine

The Revelation

F iguring out how to rid Arthur of his curse was no longer a passing fancy. It obsessed Vicki. She had to find a way. Everything that was done could be undone. Otherwise, she may truly end up as the crazy lady in the retirement home talking to a gold penis.

A thought occurred to her. Amy was into this kind of woo-woo shit. She was a regular at many of the metaphysical bookstores in the area. But Vicki pushed the idea aside. If she could handle this privately, that was optimal. Trying to figure out how to introduce her best friend to the man inside the vibrator she'd gotten her for a birthday gift was daunting.

After another week of internet searches, she started emailing psychics, self-proclaimed witches, and spiritualists. None of them were helpful. Their suggestions for breaking curses didn't work and when she tried to explain the situation on the phone, they'd hang up on her.

One night, Arthur sat on the couch as Vicki rode him softly so they could talk.

"I'm out of ideas, babe. But there's one thing left to try."

"What's that?"

"My best friend. The one who gifted you to me on my birthday. Amy. She's really into all kinds of stuff like this. She might know of a store, or something we haven't tried. Maybe she knows someone who can help."

"Why didn't you ask her about it before?"

"Well, I'm pretty sure she won't believe me. I mean, come on."

"Yeah. This is FUBARed"

"So ... to get her to believe us, we'll have to show you to her."

"Show me to her? How?"

"I have an idea. But you're going to have to be really open-minded."

Vicki opened the door.

Amy flung her arms to hug her. "I'm so glad you invited me over! I love Netflix and chill! Did you order pizza already? I'm hungry."

"No, I wanted to wait until you could tell me what you wanted."

Amy entered the townhouse and kicked off her shoes. Then an odd thing caught her eye. Two bar stools from Vicki's buffet counter stood at the back of the living room, by the kitchen, with a blanket draped between them like a barrier.

"What's this?" She indicated the structure.

Vicki tried not to blush too hard. "Well, I have something to show you. To reveal, so to speak."

"Really?" Amy sashayed over to it. "So, no peeking?"

"No. Just uh, stand by the coffee table."

"Okay." Amy assumed her position.

Vicki walked behind the sheeted area. "Are you alright?" she whispered.

Buzz.

"Think you can do this?"

Buzz.

"What's that? What's going on?" asked Amy.

Vicki nervously regarded her friend. "Yeah. This is gonna be super fucking strange. But I really need you to hang in there. You'll understand in a minute. You just have to give me a few, okay?"

"Vicki, what—"

Vicki held up the golden dildo Amy had given her. "Remember this?"

"Um. Yeah."

"Well, I found out where it came from. I found out its whole story."

"Wow! That's great. But, uh, what's going on with the, uh, blankets here?"

"That's where I need you to be patient and work with me."

"Okayyy ..."

"Be back in a sec. Just hold tight." Vicki placed Arthur's dick on one of the bar stools and hid behind the barrier to suck him.

He hardened, but not enough.

She whispered, "What's wrong?"

Buzz, buzz, buzz.

"You don't know? Are you nervous? Try to just focus on my mouth." She swooped over his tip and sucked hard, adding her hand to help him along. He began to stiffen.

Amy asked, "What are you doing, Vicki?"

Slowly, Arthur materialized. Amy jumped back.

"Oh, my God!" She clutched her heart. "What the hell?"

Arthur stood from the bar stool. Vicki unlatched and stroked him with her hand, adding lotion as they turned to face Amy. Hidden behind the blanket stretched between the bar stools from the waist down, he greeted her.

"Hi there."

Amy shrieked. By now, she'd scuttled to the front door and had a leg up against herself in terror. "What the fuck! Vicki?" Vicki stood next to Arthur with her arm still visibly moving as she jacked him behind the blanket.

"What's going on?" Amy's eyes bulged.

Vicki said, "Amy, this is Arthur. The golden dildo you bought me."

"No-no-no. This-that's-this isn't—this. What?"

"I'm Arthur," he said, starting to fade.

Vicki stroked him faster. "I'm sorry, he's a little embarrassed."

Arthur's eyes rolled back, and he solidified again. "Yeah, this is," he sighed, watching Vicki's hand on him rubbing furiously, "not your normal situation." He looked back at Amy. "I'm really sorry that we have to meet this way. But I'm cursed and it's the only way I can materialize so I can talk to people. I know it's bananas, but ... Well, here we are."

"Amy," Vicki said as she vigorously stroked Arthur to keep him corporeal. "The lady you bought him from; well, he was her great aunt's. She dabbled in the occult and stuff. Arthur told me that she hired some lady who worked in black magic to curse him so he'd have to be with her."

Amy's nervous voice wavered. "So, she turned him into a dildo?"

Arthur spoke. "She wanted to lay me, but I refused. So, she cursed me so that I'd have to. See? Down to my most basic part."

Amy lowered her leg and slumped against the door. "That's fucked up."

"You're telling me, lady!" Arthur blurted. "Now I need to figure out how to end this so I can get my life back."

"Amy, do you know a store, or a person, anyone that can help us? I've been searching the internet for weeks, and I can't find anything useful. I even called a few people, but they all hung up on me."

Amy took a few steps forward into the living room. "Yeah, uh. Well, black magic like this isn't Wiccan, Viking, Druid, or Strega. Could be Gypsy or Voodoo. I might know a place we can go to ask."

The sign said "Mama's Treasure Trove." A bell rang when Amy opened the door, and Vicki followed her inside. The shop was full of oddities for sale. It was dark inside from the dense shelves and objects that blocked the light from the windows. Inside was painted in green, yellow and black. The colors of the Jamaican flag. Red outlined the windows and doors. Vicki gaped at the bright colors and rows of packed shelves.

A woman's deep, powerful voice came from behind the glass sales counter. "Red is for protection from my enemies. No bad energy, spirit or physical, may cross my doorweh." A lovely, dark, middle-aged woman stood gracefully behind a glass counter. A multitude of long braids emerged from the back of a tie-die head wrap.

"I'm sorry. I didn't mean to stare," Vicki said timidly.

"Ah, it's okeh. What brings you leddies to my shop today?"

The pair approached the counter. The woman spread her hands along the glass countertop and leaned forward to study them.

"Something troublin' ya?" she asked.

"Yes," said Amy. "Mama Disla—"

"Mama Dee Isla. Means mother of de Island."

"I'm sorry. Mama D'Isla, we have a friend who's been cursed. We need to find a way to break it."

"Uh-huh. And what kind of curse you be dealin' wit?"

Amy motioned with a flutter of her hand to Vicki. Vicki took a deep breath and reached into her purse.

She said, "This might shock you. And I'm sorry if you think it's a bit—vulgar."

"I'd like to see the thing that shocks me!" proclaimed Mama D'Isla with a robust laugh.

Vicki pulled up Arthur. "I'm sorry," she whispered to him.

Buzz.

She pulled him from her purse and set the beautifully perfect, golden phallus on the glass countertop. "This is my friend. Arthur. He's trapped in there."

Mama D'Isla's eyes flew open wide. "Blessed saints!" she swore. "What did he do? Must have been something very bad."

"No," said Vicki. "It was plain old jealousy. A girl wanted him for herself. He refused her, so she hired a woman who practiced black magic to reduce him to this."

"Great God, Almighty! Dis is some darkness indeed." She looked closer, examining the phallus. "Ohhh," she rumbled. "My heart bleeds for dis poor soul. Him is stuck hard in dis form."

"Can you help him?" Vicki begged. "Please? I can pay you for whatever spell can reverse this."

Mama D'Isla shook her head. "No, sistah. No money can fix dis hex. Tis a dark deed been done to this man. And may their souls bear the mark for it too." She spat on the floor.

Vicki sent a panicked look to Amy.

Mama D'Isla leaned on her elbows and looked deeply into Vicki's eyes. Her face softened. "Take courage. There's always hope. Is he a good man?"

"Yes."

"Do you love 'im?"

Vicki thought about it. She'd never considered it before. Did she love Arthur? She did have feelings for him. But was it love? He was tender and beautiful. He was the best lover, and maybe even the best companion she'd ever known. She definitely had love for him. But was she in love? Honestly, she barely knew him. She did know one thing, though, she couldn't stand the idea of being without him.

"I love him," she stated plainly.

"Good. Love is the greatest weapon against evil such as this. Evil has no power in its presence. Love is the strongest force on this earth. Ya hear me?"

Vicki nodded, wide eyed.

"If ya love 'im, and love 'im true. You might have a chance."

"But is there something I can do? Some ritual or-or something?"

She shook her head again. "No. I'm sorry to say, my dear. This dark magic must run its course. When the time is right, this curse will break." Mama D'Isla took Vicki's hands in her own. "Ya must be strong, now. You'll need it. For you, and for him. Ya must be his source of strength, ya hear me? Both of ya must believe. Both of ya must love." She released Vicki's hands and stood up straight. "Only then, can ya be rid of the darkness."

Vicki looked at the limp, golden penis on the cold glass counter. "So, what you're saying is, when our love is strong enough. The curse will end?"

The woman crossed her arms and nodded. "Also, I have a special runnin' on crocodile teeth and rooster feet."

Chapter Ten

The Trash

V icki lay on her bed, softly petting the golden penis.

"Do you love me, Arthur?" she tentatively asked his sweet mushroom cap.

He remained still.

"You said you were falling for me. I realized I have some feelings, myself. Maybe there's a real chance we could break this curse."

Nothing. Not a buzz or a flinch.

"Talk to me, Arthur." She stared at his golden tip sorrowfully. "Please?"

He didn't stir for a long time. Finally, he rolled away from her, off the bed, landing on the floor with a pathetic thud. She sat up to watch him roll to her dresser. Swiveling his golden shaft, he bumped the dresser several times.

"You want to go into the drawer?"

He roll-bumped the piece of furniture once more.

Vicki went over to him and gently picked him up. "Arthur, I'm sorry we didn't get better news today. I'm sad too."

He emitted a very soft buzz.

"You need some time alone?"

Another very soft buzz.

"Alright." She kissed his shiny tip and gently placed him in her underwear drawer. "I'll check on you in a little bit." She closed the drawer halfway. "I'll leave it open so it's not too dark."

She slept by herself that night. Arthur indicated his preference to stay in the drawer. When she woke the next morning, she stared sorrowfully at the empty pillow beside her. She missed him. Her body missed him. Vicki got up and went to the drawer. Arthur was slightly curled up in a nest of her panties.

"Good morning," she greeted softly. "You awake?" She didn't hear anything, and he didn't move. "Want to come down and have coffee with me?"

Silence.

"Oh, Arthur, please stop sulking. I can't stand the thought of you in that dark drawer." She picked him up, and he immediately hopped back into the drawer. "Really? You're gonna be like that, huh?" She let out an exasperated sigh. "Fine. Wallow." She turned and went down for coffee.

An oppressive quiet enveloped her home. Without Arthur to talk to, everything felt empty. It was like being dumped all over again. She could only hope he'd recover, and they could get back to their routine. The rest of the weekend passed in a smear of dreary hours.

When Monday came, she said good morning to him in his nest of panties and went on with her morning routine. Coffee, breakfast, internet, shower. After she finished her make-up, she walked past her bedroom, and down the hall to the stairs without bothering to look into her room or underwear drawer to say goodbye to him. He'd made it clear he preferred to be alone. She grabbed her purse and left for work.

Throughout her day, Vicki could barely concentrate on her job. The small letters and numbers on her screen blurred as her mind drifted to curly, golden hair, sparkling blue eyes, and lascivious hands touching her in ways that made her feel more alive and treasured than she'd ever felt in her life.

His smile. His laugh. His heart ... *I think I really am falling in love.*

She gasped out loud.

Quickly turning off her computer, she snagged her purse and hurried through the cubicles towards the elevator. Briefly pausing at her supervisor's desk, she said, "I'm sorry, I gotta leave early today. I forgot I have a—doctor's appointment! Byeee!" She fled to the elevator before her supervisor could protest.

Anxiety jittered through her as she tried to control her speed while driving home. Every red light took a torturous eternity. She finally made it to her driveway and almost forgot to put her car in park as she launched out of the vehicle and ran to her front door. Her hand shook so badly, she dropped her keys twice, before managing to turn the lock.

"Arthur!" she called the second she was inside. She dropped her purse and ran up the stairs to her bedroom. "Arthur, I have something to tell—"

Panties hung over the edge of her underwear drawer, and several pairs were strewn around the floor. She peered inside the dresser; the remaining panties were tussled, and there was no Arthur.

"Arthur?" Dropping to her hands and knees, she searched the floor, looking in every corner and under the bed. "Arthur!" she called frantically. "Where are you?" She scanned every room for a shiny six-inch, flaccid, gold dick, but he was nowhere to be found. Not in the bathroom, not the spare room, not the stairs, the landing, the living room, or the kitchen. She even pulled her washer-dryer stack away from the wall, just in case he was hiding back there. No golden penis anywhere. She searched her kitchen once more. Nothing.

"Fuck!" In panicked frustration, she hurled a dish rag across the kitchen. It landed against her tall trash can, sending the flap at the top spinning. "The trash! Oh, my God, Arthur, please don't tell me you threw yourself away!" She opened the top of the trashcan, but the bag was brand new. "Shit, I forgot. I took the trash out this morning!"

The squeak of an airbrake outside told her the trash truck had arrived.

"No!" Vicki bolted out her front door and down the sidewalk to the dumpster.

The truck's evil claws had already secured the dumpster and were lifting it to be emptied into the back. Vicki ran to the door where the driver sat watching in his mirror preparing to dump the garbage into his truck. She frantically pounded on his door. The man startled and paused his work. His window lowered.

"What is it, lady?" he asked.

"Please, I need to get into that dumpster before you empty it! My—uh ... My niece accidentally threw out a treasured antique of mine."

"I'm sorry, lady, but I can't let you into that dumpster. It's against regulations. I could lose my job."

"Oh please, sir!" Vicki's heart hammered her ribs. "Just lower it and unhook. I'll climb in and it'll be like I did it before you even showed up!"

"But that'll put me behind schedule. Can't do that. I'll lose my bonus. Sorry."

She scrunched her face angrily. "Look, I will give you five-hundred dollars if you let me into that dumpster."

The man paused. "You got cash?"

She nodded. "Yes."

He lowered dumpster. Vicki ran to the back and waited for the man to release the levers on it.

"Hey lady! Cash first!"

She huffed and ran back to her townhouse. Under her bed, she had a lockbox with her rainy-day fund. She quickly counted out five-hundred dollars and shot back out to the asshole in the garbage truck. She handed it to him and resumed her post at the back of his stinky truck until he lowered the dumpster the rest of the way and released the clamp.

Without hesitation, and ignoring the putrid smell of vomit in the filthy thing, she flung the lids up and climbed in. *So many bags. How can I tell which is mine?* She shoved bags around until she spotted the label from the coffee pods she liked through thin plastic. A hint of gold flashed underneath the pod label.

"Gotchya!" she cried victoriously, ripping the bag open. Arthur's soft, mushroom head greeted her. "Oh, Arthur, I thought I lost you! Come here, you dumb dick." Pulling him free of the trash, she cradled his drooping girth as she carefully climbed out of the putrid metal box. "Fuck, that was disgusting."

"Hey lady!"

She turned towards the garbage man.

"I gotta know. What was so important back there?"

Vicki held out the golden schlong to him. "My Johnson!"

The man shook his head, rumbling with laughter. "Whatever. You do you, sweetheart."

She ignored him and trotted back to her townhouse. Inside, she closed the door, full of joy and laughing at herself for the story she just gave that trash guy to tell his buddies. But she didn't care. She had her Arthur back.

"Oof, you're a stinky little penis. Let's get you a bath."

In the kitchen, she filled her sink with warm, soapy water. Carefully, she washed him until the smell disappeared. "I'm so glad I came home early! Could you imagine if I'd waited till the end of my workday? You could have spent eternity in a landfill! Oh, my poor baby. Shit, you almost did before! That gal that Amy bought you from told me she almost threw you away before she decided to sell you. Ugh! I can't imagine. It's so lucky we found each other."

She rinsed him and patted him dry. "I stink too, from climbing into that dumpster. I should probably shower. But I'm not letting you out of my sight!" She carried him with her and set him on the bathroom counter so he could watch her undress and bathe herself. He seemed to harden slightly, but not completely.

After drying her body with a towel, she picked up his golden, half-woody. "Well, at least I know you're still in there." She sat him on her bed near the edge and kneeled on the floor. Laying her head on the corner of the mattress, she began petting him. "Please don't ever throw yourself away again. Promise me?"

He still didn't buzz. She reared up in agitation.

"Oh, Arthur, come on! I need to talk to you. I need to tell you something."

He rolled away from her, but she grabbed him and pointed his tip back at her.

"No. You don't get to shut me out. Not after all we've been through. Did you think that what that voodoo lady said meant you'd be stuck in this form forever? Did you think throwing yourself away would spare me somehow?" She pushed up to her feet. "Well, you're wrong, buster! I nearly lost my fucking mind when I realized you were in that trash truck! The idea of you being alone, and cold and—" She sniffed. "When you're really so alive and warm, and-and wonderful." Her eyes burned.

"I don't want to be without you. Ever." She sniffed again and crumpled back to the floor, laying an affectionate hand on his golden shaft. "Because" -sniff- "I think I'm falling for you too. And I know this is fucking strange, and you're trapped, but I don't care. I really want to give this a chance. Please, Arthur. Don't give up yet." She wiped her eyes and kissed his tip. "I'd have died if I came home from work and you were gone."

Then she perked up. "I just thought of something. Have you noticed that recently you've been able to stay a little longer? At first, you couldn't do anything at all. Then you could move on your own and even levitate! You've even materialized without me actually touching you." She stared at him hopefully. "Maybe the curse is weakening." She grabbed his shaft and lay kisses all along the ridge of his helmet.

He began to harden. Vicki adjusted herself on her knees, held him up to her mouth and wrapped her lips around his crown. Her tongue swept around as she slowly sucked him deeper into her mouth. His length expanded as he swelled.

Tenderly, she took him into her mouth all the way to the base and smoothed up and down, sucking with a passion flaming from deep in her heart. Soon, he strengthened, becoming too big for her to deep throat. Her heart danced when she heard him sigh. She clenched her eyes, squeezing out tears that streamed down her cheeks.

His warm, loving hands caressed her head as he formed and stood before her. She adjusted her kneeling position and continued sucking him. His breathing deepened. She added her hands to his girth, squeezing and pulsing them around his length. Bringing her other hand up, she gently stroked his thigh, then cupped his balls, lending just a little pressure.

"Ahhh, Victoria. That feels so good. I'm sorry about what I did. Got some strong, confusing feelings. But I thought maybe I was being selfish. How could I expect a quality dame like you to love me? Seeing as how I'm just a cock and all. How are we supposed to have a chance at a normal life? I didn't want to drag you through all that. Figured, I may as well just be trash. I'd rather be trash than hold you back."

Vicki intensified her suction on him, clasping his muscular ass. She sped her movements and listened to his sighs quicken.

"Victoria. What are you doing?"

She released him long enough to say, "Pleasing you for a change."

"Oh, God. I must be the luckiest fella around." He pressed her head with his hands as she bobbed, sucking and circling his tip with her tongue. Grunts infiltrated his sighs, and his sounds pitched up.

The spongy head she sucked swelled to a hard bulb in her mouth and heated like it could explode at any moment.

"Oh, God, Vicki, I'm gonna come." A beautiful, bellowing, crying groan flew from him.

She kept sucking with all her might until an explosion of warm cum shot into her mouth. She worked on swallowing every spurt, listening to his moans of pleasure. His hips quivered as he continued groaning.

Cum kept coming. *How much is in there?* she wondered, hoping she could swallow all of it. Then she realized that, through all their sex, he'd never once produced cum before. He'd told her that he could and did climax with her, but nothing had ever come out of him. This was real, salty, slightly bitter cum pulsing out of him.

It had to be a sign, and so Vicki breathed through her nose and kept swallowing, determined to get every drop. Finally, the throbbing knob in her mouth relaxed. She swallowed down the last of his cum and gently sucked, lightly running her hand along his shaft to see him through the end of his orgasm.

"Okay," he panted.

She released him, and he fell back onto the bed.

"Holy shit," he said through deep inhales. "That's the best damned head I ever got,"

Vicki stood and looked at him laying back on her bed, catching his breath. She really needed to rinse her mouth out, but she was astonished that he was still physically there, even with his cock turning flaccid after his climax. She'd never seen him appear without a hard-on.

"Arthur."

"Yeah."

"You're still here."

His head raised, and he looked down at his chiseled torso. "I am! Holy shit, I am! Come on and kiss me, Victoria!"

"Uh, yeah. Hang on, I need to rinse my mouth out." She raced down the hall to her bathroom, and rinsed her mouth with water and mouthwash before returning to the bed. To her delight, he was still there.

He'd moved to lay on the bed with his head on her pillows. She launched herself at him and straddled his hips, throwing her arms around him and kissing him hard. He held her, opening her mouth with his tongue and gifting her with a passionate tonsil-licker.

She stopped kissing him. "Wait. Maybe you're only still here because you haven't fulfilled your purpose. I haven't come yet."

"No way. I'm back for good. I can feel it."

"How do you know?"

"I came. For real this time. I mean, before felt good, but not like that. That was like how I remember it feeling."

She giggled. "You've never made cum before, either. Shit! Did we just break the curse with true love's first blow job?"

He gripped her body with his brawny arms and rolled her over. Settling on top of her, he stared into her eyes. "Then ... you really do love me? No foolin'?"

She smiled brightly at him. "No foolin'. I guess this means you love me too."

He blushed slightly. "Ah, shucks, Victoria. How could I not? You're the best dame a man could hope for."

He crushed her with a passionate kiss. "Whatcha got to eat around here? I'm starving. I haven't eaten in almost eighty years!"

Victoria arched a brow and spread her legs wide under him.

He grinned. "Okay. We can start with that. It's only fair." He dove down, happily licking and sucking her cunt.

Vicki almost cried again when he was still there, holding her and kissing her mouth after she climaxed. His warm, real body pressed into hers as he ran his fingers along her face.

Arthur rolled to the side and cradled her. She wrapped around him, snuggling into his muscles. She smooched every bit of skin she could reach and nuzzled into the crook of his neck with an enormous deep breath to smell him. He smelled of sweat and dish soap. A large, contented sigh floated from her.

"This. This is what I've been wanting," she said.

He squeezed her close to him with his brawny arms and peppered her forehead with kisses. "A fella could really get used to this," he replied contentedly stroking her hair.

"So," she said, "what do you want to do, now that you have your body back?"

He pensively drew a deep breath. "I want to go outside. Show me the world, Victoria."

More from Jayelle Dee

Jayelle Dee deelights in the deep and naughty! Want some more? Find her deelicious offerings here:

https://barnowlbooks.net/
https://linktr.ee/jayelledee.author
Put a little "ohhmerrgerrd" into your day!

Jayelle Dee is an exciting new author who writes classy erotic romance in contemporary settings. The stories are character driven with layers and complexity. She favors spirited female leads with attitude and a trauma that needs healing. The male leads are equally entertaining providing added personality and depth. Jayelle lives in the foothills of Colorado with her husband and their dogs.

Ring My Bell by Amelia Elliot

A Cat Shifter Reverse Harem Romance

Her kitties give her more than kisses.

Catching her narcissistic boyfriend cheating was the least surprising part of Niecy's day. That honor goes to her cats becoming men. Now she must unravel a curse that triggers whenever a bell rings. *(TW: mild domestic violence)*

Contents

Chapter One

Niecy fumbled with her front door's lock while she juggled her keys, a bag of kibble, and a gray tomcat named Johnny. Turning the deadbolt, she froze. An unusual sound came from inside her house. She strained to listen.

Johnny's bell jingled in her ear as he climbed onto her shoulder. "Shh, Johnny. Stay still." Johnny stiffened like a statue, poised to pounce. His claws dug into her skin through her blouse. Ignoring the sting, she turned the knob and crept through the door.

Slap.

There it was again. Niecy took a tentative step into the living room, her keys poking between her fingers like a weapon.

Slap.

Johnny's tail swished against her back. He made a low growl.

Slap. Slap. Slap.

The sound came from her bedroom: another slap, followed, this time, by a woman's squeal.

"Oh yes, Big Daddy! Thank you for giving me a red bottom. I'm your dirty little bunny!" Slap! "You have such big dick energy!"

Niecy's eyes narrowed. Careful not to drop Johnny, she tip-toed to the bedroom. Summoning her courage, she flung open the door, letting it slam against the wall. The doorknob made a hole in the drywall, and she winced. One more thing to repair in her century-old cottage.

Johnny leaped off her shoulder, startled by the bang, and jumped onto the nearby dresser. Free of her passenger, Niecy rushed into the bedroom to confront its occupants.

"Preston! I knew you were cheating! Who's your slut?"

The woman on her knees in front of Preston jumped to her feet, wearing nothing but a collar with a chain leash, a pair of pink thigh-high stockings, and bunny ears.

Niecy staggered to a stop. Her mouth went dry. "Alyssa?" Her legs wobbled. "You're—you're fucking my sister?" She covered her eyes with her hands. "Oh my God, Lissy! Put some fucking clothes on! I don't want to see your cooch!"

Fabric rustled. "Niecy! I can explain!" Alyssa cried.

"I wasn't expecting you for another two hours," Preston said, his voice irritatingly calm.

"How long has this been going on?" Niecy screeched, ignoring Preston. "He's my fiancé! We've been together since college. How could you possibly explain?" Tears gathered in her eyes behind her hand, and she felt dizzy.

"Niecy, look at me!" Alyssa begged.

Niecy's face scrunched in disgust. "Are you still naked?"

"No. I have a sheet on."

Niecy dropped her hand, letting the tears fall down her cheeks. "*My* sheet. In *my* house. In *my* bedroom. Now I'm going to have to burn it!"

Alyssa began to sob. "I'm sorry, Niecy. I didn't mean to. It just happened. I didn't know how to tell you."

"How long?" Niecy demanded.

Alyssa sniffed. "Does it matter?"

"How fucking long?" Niecy yelled.

"Three months," Alyssa whispered.

"Three months! You've been sneaking around my back for three months?" She threw the bag of cat food at Alyssa.

Preston batted it down and it crashed on the floor, its contents spilling and rolling across the hardwood. "Get control of yourself, Eunice." He looked down his nose at her, like he always did.

"Control myself?! Fuck you, Preston!" She lunged at him with her keys, aiming for his stupid, arrogant, cheating ball-sack.

Easily quicker than Niecy's chubby, non-athletic five-foot-two frame, Preston side-stepped her. Just as quickly, he raised his hand and slapped her so hard on her cheek that her head snapped around, and she saw stars. She stumbled backward several steps, falling to her knees.

"I told you to calm down," he sneered.

Alyssa gasped. "Niecy, are you okay?"

From the corner of her eye, Niecy watched Alyssa scrambling to dress. She was okay—well, except for her sister betraying her. Preston had never raised a hand to her before, but she wasn't surprised. Just like she knew he would cheat, she knew he was capable of violence. And, in fairness, she'd been going for his nuts.

Before Niecy could say anything, Johnny launched off the dresser, claws bared, straight at Preston's head. Hissing, his fur standing on end, Johnny resembled an alien face-hugger.

Preston screamed and slapped at Johnny. "Fucking dirty stray!" Grabbing Johnny by the scruff, Preston flung him across the room. Stripes of blood bloomed across Preston's face from where

Johnny's claws had dug into his cheeks. "I'm going to have to go to the hospital and get a rabies shot," Preston whined.

Still kneeling on the floor, Niecy wiped her tears and glared at Preston. "Johnny's vaccinated. Anyway, those are scratches not bites. Clean them and you'll be fine. Don't be such a douche."

"Johnny's hurt." Alyssa rushed to where Niecy's cat laid slumped on the floor to check him.

"Alyssa, leave it," Preston barked.

Alyssa stiffened, stepping away from the cat. "Yes, sir."

"These scratches better not leave any scars, or I'll have that animal destroyed." Preston sniffed in derision, wiping his finger along the dots of blood on his cheek.

"Leave my cats alone." Niecy tried to sound defiant, but her voice wavered. Preston's father was the mayor, and his mother was the town judge. She knew he could round up all her cats and have them euthanized if he wanted. "They're innocent animals."

"They're worthless fleabags, and the only one who'd miss them is you." Preston stepped up to her and glowered at her from above. "Do you know why I'm leaving you, Eunice?"

She didn't care, so she didn't bother to answer.

He raised his eyebrows. "It's simple. You're beneath me. I've given you plenty of chances. But all you want to do after work is rescue these disgusting stray cats, fix up this piece of shit house, and read your girl-porn."

Preston was correct that her house and her job were her priorities. Niecy had inherited the property, and all the stray cats, from her deceased parents two years ago. After decades of neglect, the house needed a ton of work and Niecy had to do it all herself.

And it's not like Preston would dirty his hands to help. He was far too good for manual labor.

After work, Niecy moonlighted as a do-it-yourselfer. She couldn't afford a contractor because her job paid little, as she was completing her fieldwork for her license in clinical social work. Alyssa got the cash from their parents' meager life insurance policies instead of a part of the house. They'd agreed that Alyssa would use the money to finish college, but she'd dropped out last semester and got a job at the local coffee shop instead.

Was that Preston's fault? Looking at him through her waterlogged vision, anger roiled Niecy's stomach. She mumbled, "get out of my house."

She wouldn't miss him. What little time she allocated for relaxation, she spent playing with her cats and reading smutty novels in the bath, just as he said. Preston was a selfish, neglectful lover, so steamy books and her vibrator were the only way she'd gotten off in years. Having her needs met by her book boyfriends, she paid little attention to what he did or where he went, which was probably why it was so easy for him to cheat on her.

"Furthermore"—he wasn't done berating her—"we've lived together for over a year. I reluctantly moved into this hovel because you begged me. But when I come home after a long day at work, where is my dinner? Where is my clean house? Where is my adoring girlfriend from when we were in college? Outside playing with parasite-ridden feral cats like a mentally deficient child."

He was correct about that, too, more or less; she'd stopped doting on him like she did in college. Back then, she thought he was superior, and she was grateful he was with her. She put in a lot of effort to keep him, catering to his every whim and flattering him constantly. She'd adored him, once. And he adored being adored.

Preston's lip curled in disgust. "Look at you in your yoga pants, even though you never do yoga. They're called yoga pants, not cookie dough pants." He huffed. "You don't make an effort anymore. I started dating you because you had potential, and you showed me you were willing to work for it. Then your parents died, and you stopped trying. I've been patient, but it's gone on too long. You could never be my wife. It's cute you even thought that."

She thought that because, after her parents' funeral, possibly to stop her crying, he got down on one knee and asked her. She said yes, thinking he was the best she could ever do, but he'd never bought her a ring. She'd known for a year and a half they weren't heading for happily ever after, and moving in together wasn't the fix she'd hoped it would be.

Niecy shrunk into a ball, a searing pain ripping a hole in her chest. She'd been prepared for months to live alone with her cats, but she hadn't expected him to steal her sister. "Get out of my house," she repeated.

"Gladly." He turned to Alyssa. "Get your things, bunny. We can stay in my parent's pool house. It's a thousand times better than this place, anyway."

Rage turned Niecy's vision red. "Get. The fuck. Out."

"You're pathetic." Preston sneered at her as he stepped over her. "I'll come back for my things tomorrow. You better not damage anything, or I'll take you to court and seize this house to pay for it." He waited for Alyssa, wrapping a protective arm around her waist when she got to his side.

"Niecy," Alyssa said softly from the doorway. "I'm sorry."

"You have nothing to apologize for, bunny. Be proud that you're my woman. You've earned it." Preston glanced over his shoulder at Niecy, who hadn't moved from where she kneeled on the floor, her shoulders hunched. "Take a lesson from your sister, Niecy. Without drastic changes, you're going to die alone, with nothing but your cats and pornographic novels to keep you company. For your sake, I hope you think long and hard about that."

"Don't threaten me with a good time," she shouted as she heard the front door click in its jam.

Too emotionally overwrought to stand, Niecy crawled to where Johnny laid on the floor, slipping on the strewn cat food. Johnny hadn't moved since Preston had tossed him against the wall. "Please don't be dead," she whispered, her heart squeezing.

She let out a tiny sigh of relief when she saw Johnny's side move. She smoothed her hands over his body, gingerly lifting him until he was cradled, limp in her arms. "Please don't be hurt." Niecy's heart somersaulted when Johnny stretched, his green eyes blinking as they focused on her. He began to purr.

She squeezed him against her chest. "Oh my God, Johnny! I was so scared. I love you so much. But never do that again! Preston's spiteful, and I don't know what I'd do without you." Her tears fell anew as she stood and brought him to the bed, setting him on her stomach as she laid back on the mattress. "I can't believe I dated that asshole for five years."

Still purring, Johnny crawled up her chest until his nose pressed against her lips. He batted at her cheek with a soft paw. "Oh, you want a kiss?" She puckered her lips and kissed the wet tip of his nose.

Suddenly, her entire body was pinned under a heavy weight—it was like a dead body landed on her.

No. Not a dead body. A very much alive body. A man!

Surprised, Niecy shrieked. "Please don't hurt me!"

The man jerked.

Niecy heard Johnny's bell ring. Where was her cat? Did the man crush him?

Then, just as suddenly as he'd appeared, the man was gone, and she was alone on the bed, with Johnny on her chest.

She looked around her room. It was empty, and the window was closed. The house was completely silent. "What the fuck? Am I hallucinating?" Niecy wiped a hand over her face. Maybe emotional stress was causing her to mentally crack.

Johnny purred loudly in her face. He nosed her mouth.

"Not now, baby." She absentmindedly ran her hand from the top of his head to his tail. "I need to think."

Johnny batted at her lips with his paw. Then he nosed her again.

"Stop it." She moved her face to the side.

Grabbing her cheek with his claw, Johnny guided her face back to him. Then he nosed her mouth.

"Okay, okay. You want kisses." She puckered her lips, pecking his nose.

Then she was under the man again. She screamed.

The man jumped off her, his hand clutching something at his throat. "Niecy! Stop screaming! It's me, Johnny."

Chapter Two

"Johnny?" The man was stark naked. Niecy felt like she might faint. "What do you mean, you're Johnny?" She pinched her forearm. "Ow! I'm not dreaming. Wait, I should try again. Maybe I'm just dreaming it hurt." She pinched her forearm again, digging her fingernails into the skin. "Ow!"

"Niecy, calm down. It really is me." He took a hesitant step toward the bed. "Look, I'll show you my collar with the tag. But you must be very careful to not ring my bell."

Niecy's eyes bugged out as she stared at him. The back of her mind noticed the naked man was supremely hot, but the front of her mind was busy panicking. "What's happening?" She let out a long, tortured moan. "Oh my God, I've gone crazy. I'm never going to get my license as a social worker now. They're going to commit me. Five years to get my masters. Two years of fieldwork. I'm going to lose it all." She tugged on her hair with both hands.

The naked man three feet from her sighed. "You're not going crazy."

"Oh yes, I am. Go away, please." She squeezed her eyes shut and counted to ten. "Are you gone yet?"

"No."

She opened one eye and peeked at him. He hadn't moved a muscle, despite having so many of them. "Why not?"

"Because you're not going crazy. And because we need to talk." He took another hesitant step forward. "Please, Niecy. Just hear me out."

She sat up and drew her knees to her chest. "Okay, fine. You might as well explain yourself. You're just my subconscious, anyway. I'm sort of curious what my deeply disturbed mind has concocted."

His expression was pained. "I'll start with the short version. About a hundred years ago, I was cursed into cat form. When someone who truly loves me kisses me, I return to my human form. So, thank you." He pushed shaggy brown hair off his forehead. "But whenever a bell rings, I revert to my cat form. My collar is enchanted and cannot be removed, and the bell rings whenever I move, so I'm in cat form ninety percent of the time."

Niecy squinted at him, trying to understand the rules of his curse. "What about the other ten percent of the time?"

"Whenever I'm on consecrated ground, like in a church, the curse loses its power. But since I can't wear clothes, that isn't very often. Sometimes I go to the abandoned chapel, just to remember what it's like to be human. You can always take me there, no matter what, and I'll return to human form."

"Why can't you wear clothes? Is that part of the curse? Like does your skin burn if you put them on?"

"What?" He chuckled. "No. I'm just not big enough to carry them around when I'm a ten-pound cat."

"Oh." She relaxed her shoulders, studying him. "How do I know you're really Johnny, and not just some weirdo who likes to wear collars with a tag that says the name of my cat? I mean, he's a gray cat, and you don't even have gray hair. You could be a stalker."

"I'll show you. I'll ring my bell and you'll see me change into a cat instantly. Then kiss me, and I'll change back just as quickly."

"Okay." She scooted to the end of the bed. "Show me."

He hesitated. "You must promise to kiss me right away. I don't want to be a cat. Please promise you'll keep me as a man for a while. You have no idea how bad cat food tastes, and mice are even worse. The only half-decent thing cats eat are birds. That's why they kill so many of them."

Taking a deep breath, she stood and moved close to him, peering into his eyes. They were the same striking shade of green as her cat's. "Okay." Maybe he was her Johnny, and he'd intentionally attacked Preston earlier for her. The least she could do was let him eat proper food for dinner tonight. "I promise. You won't be a cat for more than a few seconds."

"Thank you." He stepped back from her. "Ready?"

"Yes."

He dropped his hand from his throat and shook his head. The bell rang. Before the sound had left her ears, the naked man was gone, and in his stead sat Johnny, her cat.

He was telling the truth. She saw it with her own eyes. Although she still couldn't rule out psychosis, she decided that believing her cat was really an enchanted hunk was far better.

She bent down and picked him up, placing him on the edge of the bed. "Stay seated there. I'll kiss you and, that way, you won't crush me when you change back."

Johnny meowed.

Squatting before the mattress, she puckered her lips and leaned toward her cat. He nosed her mouth. No sooner did her mouth connect with his nose than he switched into a man. And so, just as suddenly, she found herself looking straight at his lap—or, more precisely, she was eye-to-eye with his one-eyed snake, her still-puckered lips grazing the tip.

Leaning back only an inch, she stared at his dick. It rose under her gaze. It was a nice cock, as far as cocks go, growing to an appealing girth and length. It was far nicer than Preston's skinny prick. As it'd been years since she'd seen a quality male appendage in the flesh, she licked her lips.

Why was she staring at his dick? "Oh my God. Sorry!" Niecy popped up. She stumbled back a few steps, trying to regain her composure.

"Do you believe me now?"

"Uh, yeah. Yes," she stammered, flushing red from her neck to her ears. "Yes. I believe you."

Keeping one hand on his bell, he reached for a pillow and placed it on his lap. "Is that better?"

She bit her lip, blushing even harder. "Mm-hmm," she squeaked. She tried to focus. "So you've been a cat most of the time for a hundred years?"

"Yes."

"Is your name really Johnny? Or is that your cat name?"

"It's my real name."

"When's the last time someone kissed you back into a man?"

"You're the first."

"Really?"

"Really." He smiled softly. "I fell in love with you two years ago. I expected to love you as a cat until you became suspicious that I was living longer than a cat should." His smile broadened. "I can't believe you loved me back enough to return me to human form."

She slow-blinked as his words sunk in. "You—you love me?"

"With all my heart, my darling. That's why I never leave your side when you're home."

Her mind raced as she listened to him. She didn't think any man had loved her before—not even Preston—and Johnny had been a cat until recently. "How? You hardly know me."

"I've known you your whole life, Niecy. I saw you as a little girl, playing in the trees around the old church and taking care of your sister. I saw you leave for college as a girl and return as a grown, magnificent woman. I see you take care of this house, and the unloved people in town, and all the abandoned cats, every day."

"You do?" She sucked in a sharp breath. "Does that mean, while you're a cat, you can understand everything I'm saying and doing?"

"Yes. I can even watch TV and use your computer. I learned to type from walking on your keyboard while you were working. I have my own G-mail account. Of course, I had to type nonsense when you were around so you wouldn't get suspicious."

"Wow." She laughed, relaxing into his company. "I can't believe this. Since you're always with me, maybe you know me better than anyone."

"Yes, my darling." He nodded. "Another thing I know for sure: Preston is a massive douchebag."

Niecy snickered. "Yup. He's a douchenozzle."

"A douchewagon."

"Douchehat."

"Douchelord."

"That's a good one," she said with a snort. "Douchecicle."

"Douchenuts," Johnny offered with a snicker.

"Douchenoggin."

"Wait." Johnny held up a hand. "I got the perfect one. Preston is a Douche McGouche."

Niecy choked on a laugh.

Johnny laughed, too, but then his smile faded. "I've hated that guy from Day One. He was never good enough for you. I could smell other women on him besides your sister. Promise me you won't let him worm his way back into your life."

"No chance of that." She pulled a face. "I can't believe he's talked so many women into fucking him. Not only is he an asshole, he's terrible at sex. I don't know why I was with him for so long. I can't even blame it on being dickmatyzed. I haven't had good sex, or even mediocre sex, in years."

"I haven't had sex at all in a century," Johnny replied, his tone flat.

"Okay, you win." She wrinkled her nose, looking at his fist clutched to his throat. "When's the last time you've had cookie dough?"

"I snuck a few licks of the spoon the last time you made cookies. Why?"

"Wait here. I've got an idea."

She sprinted into the kitchen and retrieved a tub of pre-made cookie dough from the refrigerator. She pulled open the lid and was forming a small ball of dough in her fingers by the time she'd returned to her bedroom. "Open up," she said.

He opened his mouth. She placed the ball of dough on his tongue.

He groaned in appreciation. "Wow, that's good," he mumbled as he chewed. Using two fingers, he scooped more out of the bucket and fed it to her. "Have some."

She sucked it off his fingers, letting the creamy, sugary mix melt on her tongue. He went back for seconds. Watching him savor the dough, she reveled in the pleasure on his face. She put that smile on his lips, and that made her smile reflexively. Rolling another ball of cookie dough between her index finger and thumb, she scooted in close. "Take your hand off the bell and stay very still."

He eyed her curiously but didn't argue. Dropping his hand, he didn't move while she shoved the cookie dough into the bell on his collar.

She stepped back to admire her handiwork. "That should gum it up for a little bit so you can move. We'll have to figure out a more permanent solution later." She grinned.

"Thank you!"

"You're welcome." But no sooner had those words left her lips than her phone chimed with an incoming text and Johnny became a cat again. She frowned while he climbed out from under the pillow that he'd had on his lap.

"Oh, shoot. This is going to be annoying." She dug out her phone. The text was from Alyssa. "Nope. After what she did, she's getting blocked." Niecy put her phone on silent, with the emergency bypass set to vibrate only.

She looked at Johnny where he sat on the bed in cat form. "If I lay down and have you kiss me, you'll crush me. If I pick you up and kiss you, I'll drop you. I think I have to kiss you while you're sitting down."

Johnny meowed his agreement.

Squatting in front of him, she closed her eyes and pursed her lips. When she opened them again, his fully erect dick brushed against her mouth. She liked it. Without moving away, she looked up at him. "Would you like to experience sex again? Or would that be weird, given that you're my cat and all?"

"I'm not really a cat," he pointed out. "I'm a man."

She traced her tongue around the crown of his cock, thrilling at how his breath caught. "Indeed, you are." And he wasn't any mere man. He was an incredibly sexy man, with a rock-hard cock and rock-hard abs to match. It was as though one of her book boyfriends had come to life and was eager to lay some pipe, not caring one iota about her thick thighs, squishy tummy, and yoga pants.

And he wanted to eat cookie dough with her. She licked her lips.

She wondered which was more insane: having sex with her cursed shifter cat or having sex with her hallucination. He stroked his engorged cock right before her eyes, and she decided she didn't care. She needed a good dicking down after years of unsatisfying sex with Preston.

Mind made up, she stood and pulled her T-shirt over her head.

Chapter Three

"I like watching you undress," Johnny said, leaning back against the headboard. "I've seen it hundreds of times, but I never get sick of it. You're so beautiful."

Niecy hesitated. It hadn't bothered her to get undressed in front of her cat before, but that's because she thought he was a cat. She was suddenly self-conscious as Preston's mocking words rang in her head. She was a curvy woman who'd indulged in cookie dough too much, and yoga too little. Her rounded belly and limbs were proof. She pressed her arms across her stomach, trying to conceal her squish.

"Don't be shy, my darling." Johnny jumped from the bed and stood before her. His movements were athletic, lithe, graceful, like a panther. "Let me help you." He placed his hands on her hips. "That might even be better. It's a rare treat for me to undress a woman, much less a goddess."

A goddess? She blushed. "Alright, then."

He took his time, running his hands over every inch of her skin as he removed her bra first. When her torso was bare, he sunk to his knees and sucked on her breasts. He worshiped her nipples until she whimpered and trembled. And he left hickeys on the tender, pale flesh.

"Can I tell you a secret?" he asked. His fingers inched the waistband of her yoga pants downward while he lapped at the skin of her belly and sprinkled love bites over her hipbones.

She stood stock still, letting him experience her body however he pleased. "What's that?" she answered after a long pause, her words breathy.

"All those times you were reading when I sat on your shoulder ... I was reading along with you. I know all the dirty things you've read about. I know the scenes that turned you on until you reached your hand between your legs and stroked yourself to orgasm." As he spoke, his fingers slid under the elastic band on her panties and grazed the skin hooding her clit.

She gasped, impatience overshadowing any self-consciousness. "Take my pants off. That'll make it easier for you to touch me there."

"I know, my darling. I haven't forgotten how to make love to a beautiful woman." But he didn't yet disrobe her. "I'm going to take my time, savoring every inch of you. You're the most delectable treat I've had in a century, or perhaps in my entire life."

Tasting her skin, he eased her yoga pants down, inch by maddening inch, until they were bunched around her knees. Crawling behind her, he sunk his teeth softly into the ample flesh of her ass while he rubbed a finger over her panties, stroking her labia from behind through the thin cotton. "You're so wet already," he murmured. "My perfect, sexy, beautiful goddess."

Niecy's thighs shook at his soft touch. She feared she would beg for him to fuck her soon. Biting the inside of her cheek, she closed her eyes and let him take her on his sensual ride.

Then his hand was gone. Her eyes flew open, and a small squeak bubbled from the back of her throat. Instead of continuing to tease her with his hands and mouth, he picked her up by the waist and tossed her onto the bed like she weighed nothing. "What—?"

"Shh." With a yank, he pulled her yoga pants off her, leaving her bare except her sensible cotton panties. A noise like a growl rumbled through his chest as he climbed onto the bed next to her. Lifting her leg over his shoulder, he licked the back of her knee. Then he slowly nibbled, kissed, and tickled his way up her inner thighs.

Coaxing her legs wider, he pressed his nose to her pussy and breathed deep. Then he licked at the wet spot on the gusset of her panties, pushing the cotton inside her with his tongue.

She shivered. "Johnny," she said his name in a sigh. "Johnny. I can't wait any longer. Please. I need you inside me."

Shoving the cotton of her panties to the side, he slipped a finger into her pussy. "Will that do?"

She moaned, lost for words.

He stroked his finger along her g-spot. Then he added a second. Then a third. He stretched her and filled her until her hips began to move of their own accord.

"Oh, Johnny." She threaded her hands in his hair and arched her back off the mattress.

Pulling his fingers out of her pussy, she watched him lick her arousal off them with the flat of his tongue. "You taste so good, my darling. So sweet." Pushing on to his knees, he hooked his fingers on the waistband of her panties and slowly slid them down her legs. "I'm going to feast on your beautiful cunt until you come all over my face. And even then, I may not stop."

She trembled as he lowered onto his elbows between her thighs and took long, slow laps, back to front, back to front. The tip of his tongue flicked at her clit while he worked his fingers back inside her. He sucked on her and teased her, humming in delight and taking his time, giving her the best head she'd ever experienced.

When she came, it lasted so long she swore time stopped. He continued to lap up her arousal long after her orgasm had receded, and she was left twitching.

Sitting up, he licked his lips. "You're better than I'd imagined, and, trust me, I'd imagined it a lot." He moved up her body, stopping briefly to suck on her taut nipples, before kissing her passionately. She got lost in the heady sensation of his kiss, all her muscles relaxing into a puddle on the mattress. Then he embraced her tightly and rolled her until he was on his back and she laid on top of him.

She stiffened, self-conscious again. "Am I crushing you?" Surely, she was too heavy.

He laughed an easy laugh. "Are you kidding? I could lie with you on top of me forever." He stroked his hands up and down her spine. "But what I really want right now is for you to straddle me. I want to watch your insanely sexy body bouncing on my cock. I could come just thinking about it."

She flushed. "I don't usually like being on top."

"You'll like it with me," he said. "I promise."

Since this was probably all in her imagination, she had no reason to be embarrassed. She bit her lip and sat on her knees. She stroked his thick cock a few times, but he didn't need any priming. Poised with him lined up at her entrance, she paused, realizing he was bare.

She never fucked new partners bare. She was a social worker, for goodness' sake.

"You haven't had sex in a century?" she asked.

"That's right. So I'm not sure how long I'll last. My balls are pretty full."

She snickered. "No. I just mean ... Well, I guess you've had all the blood tests when I took you to the vet a few months back, and there was no sign of infection, so you must be clean."

She'd saved up to neuter him, too, along with several other cats on the property. But whenever she'd made an appointment, he'd disappear for days. That made sense now. "Luckily, I haven't had you snipped yet." She grinned. "I'm on the pill."

Mind made up, she widened her knees and took his cock inside her. "Mmm, wow, you're a perfect fit."

His eyes shut and he sighed. "I'd forgotten how good that feels." He opened his eyes again, giving her an intense smolder. "Ride me, Niecy. Use me for your pleasure. I want to see you fall apart on my dick."

She moved, swiveling her hips back and forth and throwing her head back. The bellend of his cock pressed against her g-spot as she rode him, and the root created friction against her clit. Pressure built in her lower belly as another orgasm brewed. Despite her desire to go wild on top of him, she kept her pace slow and measured because she worried about her heavy natural tits flopping all over the place.

"Goddamn, you're beautiful." He gripped handfuls of her ass. "So curvy, with your big breasts, big hips, and little waist. You're like a pin up." His hips pumped into her, taking control of their pace, and his words came out as breathy grunts.

She liked being compared to a pin up. Letting go of her inhibitions, surrendering to the pleasure, she met his speed, thrust for thrust. She cried out with every slam of his cock. "Fuck me, Johnny. That's it. Fill me up." Her thighs burned from exertion and sweat beaded between her breasts.

Moving his hands to her hips, aiding her as she grew tired, he used his powerful arms to lift her and slam her down ever faster. "Niecy, my darling. I need you to come. Come for me now. I can't hold back."

"I'll come if you come." She slid her hand down her belly and flicked her clit while he pounded into her.

His eyes widened as he watched her pleasure herself. "Jesus fucking Christ, you're sexy." He jerked, then thrusted hard into her, a long groan escaping his lips. His orgasm triggered hers and she swayed wildly on top of him, her loud cries echoing through the cottage.

Soon they slowed, and she stopped to admire his sweat-slicked torso. "You're one beautiful man, Johnny," she purred. She folded at the waist and rested her cheek on his shoulder. They were both hot, sticky, and panting, but she didn't care. That was easily the best sex she'd ever had, and she needed a moment.

After a while, her legs cramped. Reluctantly, she lifted off his cock, which was impressively still semi-hard, and stretched out next to him. His cum pooled between her thighs, running down her legs and on to the sheets. "We made a mess," she said. "You weren't kidding that you had a big load to give me." She shifted, trying to avoid making a wet spot, but failing. She sighed. "I need to clean up. Want to take a shower with me?"

"I would love to take a shower. You have no idea how much I miss those. But ..." he pointed at the cookie dough encrusted bell on his collar.

She twisted her mouth as she considered his problem. "It'll be alright. I'll cover your collar in plastic wrap. That should protect it."

Twenty minutes later, after she'd used half a roll of plastic to sheathe his bell, she was bent over with her knee hitched on the sink. She watched him in the mirror, fucking her vigorously. She ogled the cut muscles on his body straining and flexing with every thrust. His hardness stood in relief to her softness while he pummeled her, and she moaned her pleasure.

Sweeping her brown hair into a ponytail in his fist, making it easier for her to see him, his eyes caught hers in the reflection. "You won't be able to walk by the time I'm done with you," he promised, a snarl curling his lips as he came.

She didn't care. Walking was overrated. She wanted to spend the next week fucking him. She had some accrued vacation time, and she couldn't think of a better use for it.

Chapter Four

A car door slammed, jarring Niecy awake. She lifted her head off the sofa, where she sprawled naked on a towel. "Johnny?"

"It's Douche McGouche and your sister." He stood by the window, peeking through the curtains, the mid-morning sun cutting shadows across the floor. "He's come for his things."

"Oh shit!" She'd been so busy getting busy with Johnny, she'd completely forgotten about Preston. She jumped off the couch and ran to the bedroom to throw on a T-shirt and yoga pants.

The doorbell rang. She twirled and hopped back into the living room while she pulled on her pants. "Johnny!" Skidding to a stop behind the couch, she spun in a panic, looking for him. He sat on the windowsill, returned to cat form. "Oh, Johnny. I'll turn you back as soon as they leave, okay?"

"Meow."

"I know you're in there Eunice." Preston pounded on the door and rang the doorbell several more times. "Hurry up. I don't have all day."

As soon as she opened it, he pushed past her. Alyssa followed, whispering to Niecy, "I tried to text you to tell you when we were coming."

Preston stopped midway into the living room and looked around, puzzlement on his face. "Where are the boxes of my things?"

Niecy blinked. "Did you expect me to pack your shit for you?"

"You didn't?" He looked completely shocked. "What else did you have to do last night?"

She thought about telling him she was having the best sex of her life, all night long, but bit her tongue.

Preston snapped at Alyssa. "Go pack my stuff, bunny. And be quick about it. I have a tee time in an hour."

"Yes, sir." Alyssa hopped out of the room. She paused in the hallway leading from the living room to the bedroom. "Niecy, do you have any boxes?"

Niecy crossed her arms. "Nope."

Alyssa looked at Preston. "What would you like me to do, my king?"

King? Niecy audibly retched.

Preston scoffed. "Useless, both of you." He stuck his tongue in his cheek as he thought about it. "I'm going to go play golf. I'll leave you here, Alyssa, to take care of this. I expect everything to be packed up and ready to go when I return."

Alyssa blinked. "But I won't have a car. How am I supposed to get boxes?"

"Niecy can drive you to the hardware store." He rolled his eyes. "Jesus, it's not that hard. It's a good thing I don't need you to think, so long as you can cook and bear pretty babies."

Alyssa turned to Niecy, pleading in her eyes.

She really didn't want to help Alyssa, but Alyssa was still her sister. "Fine."

Preston reached into his back pocket and handed Niecy a folded document. "I've got an order here from the town judge to round up that beast you call Johnny and have him destroyed as a dangerous animal."

Niecy snatched the document from Preston. "You mean, you cried to your mother about a minor scratch from a ten-pound kitty cat and got her to abuse her power?" She glared at him. "You can't have him. Not now. Not ever."

Preston rolled his eyes. "I don't need your help." He took a step toward the windowsill. "I'll round up the little fleabag myself. Here, kitty, kitty. I won't hurt you."

Johnny arched his back and hissed.

"No!" Niecy launched herself at Preston, hopping onto his back and covering his ears with her hands. "Johnny, run!"

"Meow!"

"Don't argue with me. I'll be fine. But you're too small to defend yourself."

"Meow!"

"Please! Go to the church! I'll come find you!"

Johnny jumped out the window and sprinted across the yard and into a copse of trees.

Preston bucked liked a bronco with his nuts cinched and tossed Niecy off his back. He spun to face her, the veins in his neck popping. "What the fuck is wrong with you? I had no idea you were such a crazy bitch!"

She scrambled across the floor like a crab, looking for something, anything, she could use to defend herself. She snatched the half-empty bucket of cookie dough off the coffee table and chucked it at Preston, followed by a dirty plate, a pillow that'd fallen off the sofa, and a can of Cheez Whiz.

The can connected with his forehead. "Ow! What the fuck, Niecy? Have you lost your ever-lovin' mind? Jealousy is not a good look on you. Get over it, already. I don't want you anymore."

"Want me? I don't want you! You're a Douchey McDoucherson!" Niecy shouted. "You suck in bed, and your dick is tiny!"

Fury crossed his face, making him red and ugly. How'd she ever think his curly blond hair and Patrician features were handsome? He might be twenty-five, but he looked boyish, and skinny, and ... *snobby*.

"You're the one who sucks. You're a cold fish." He picked up the Cheez Whiz and chucked it back at her with a grunt from his exertion. Niecy ducked and the Cheez Whiz crashed against the wall behind her, the top popping off and splattering salty orange goo all over her hair and a framed picture of her staring adoringly at Preston.

"Now look what you did!" Niecy huffed. "Douchemonkey!" She stuck her fingers into her hair and found it to be a sticky mess. She cringed at the cheese all over the wall and floor. How was there so much? Last night, Johnny had been spraying Cheez Whiz straight into his mouth with such gusto Niecy was surprised any remained.

Preston smirked. "Serves you right." He looked at his Rolex. "I don't have time to deal with your antics, Niecy. Alyssa, I'll be back in about five hours. See that everything is on the porch, so I don't have to come back in and deal with Sybil here. Round up that cat while you're at it." He spun on his heel and marched out the front door.

Niecy turned to look at Alyssa, whose mouth hung open. Her eyes were enormous. "Niecy?"

"What?"

"Did you just have a conversation with your cat?"

Not trusting Alyssa with her secrets—even though she was dying to tell her, honestly—Niecy scowled. "You better get to work, bunny. My car keys are on the kitchen counter so you can go get boxes. I'm taking a bath." She brushed by Alyssa and headed to her bathroom, locking the door behind her, but cracking the window in case Johnny was around. She heard Alyssa leave while she ran the water.

After washing the worst of the Cheez Whiz out of her hair, she settled deeper into the bathtub. Johnny didn't jump through the window, but two of her other cats did: a black cat named Thomas and an orange cat named Harry. That was no surprise. Thomas and Harry frequently followed her to the bathroom and watched her bathe.

Thomas sat at the end of the tub, his eyes never leaving her. Harry laid flat along the side, his paws over both edges, the right front paw skimming the warm water. He yawned and purred.

Niecy smiled. "Hey, babies." She scooted to scratch them both under their chins. "Have you seen Johnny?"

Of course, neither of them answered. Maybe she really was cracking up, thinking she could talk to her cats. But being with Johnny felt so real. They fucked half the night, got a few hours' sleep, and started again at first light. Then they ate toaster waffles with whipped cream and fruit for breakfast, and she rode him on the sofa while he licked maple syrup off her nipples.

Excitement rushed through her pussy at the memory. How was she so turned on again? Johnny had revved her libido to an eleven out of ten. It's like five years of unsatisfied desire had bubbled up to the surface in one night, turning her into some kind of sex monster.

On the corner of her tub sat her waterproof vibrator. She kept it there because she used it often, even when Preston was in the adjacent bedroom. Two-pump Preston never noticed her using it, or that it sat so blatantly in the open. He also never realized why she always took long baths after they had sex.

Biting her lip, she glanced around the bathroom. Alyssa had returned, and Niecy could hear her working in the bedroom, packing Preston's wardrobe. *Preston. Ick.* She stuck her tongue out in disgust.

Pushing Preston out of her mind, she thought about Johnny instead. Switching on her vibrator, she dipped it under the surface of the water. She pressed it to her clit and closed her eyes, remembering hard muscles, an Energizer Bunny dick, and shaggy brown hair.

She sighed as the tension between her legs built. A soft paw touched her cheek. Her eyes fluttered open. Thomas perched on the corner of the tub, balanced precariously over the water to reach her face. He brushed her lips and purred.

As he pulled back to steady himself on the tub's ledge, his bell tinkled. Niecy turned off her vibrator and sat up. Leaning closer to Thomas, she looked at his collar. It looked just like the one Johnny wore. She'd never noticed that before. "Thomas," she whispered, "can you understand me?"

"Meow."

Her heart skittered in her chest.

"Meow." That time, it was Harry who spoke. He stood on the edge of the tub, gingerly walking closer to her. His collar was identical to Johnny's and Thomas's.

"Harry, are you and Thomas like Johnny?"

"Meow."

She held her hand out to Harry. "Tap your paw twice on the back of my hand if you can understand me."

Tap. Tap.

Her hand flew to her mouth. "Oh my God." She held out her other hand to Thomas.

Tap. Tap.

She gasped. How many of the stray cats on her property were actually men? How did this happen? She flexed her hand in front of Thomas. "Are there more than the three of you? Tap once for yes, twice for no."

Tap. Tap.

Before she could sigh in relief, she needed to verify the answer. "Harry, is it just the three of you? Once for yes, twice for no." She held her hand to him.

Tap.

"So every other cat is actually just a cat?"

Tap.

"Oh my God." She stood up in a rush, whooshing the water and splashing Harry, but he didn't jump off. In fact, neither Harry nor Thomas ever appeared afraid of water. She pressed a hand to her breast. "Do you guys want to be men again?"

"Meow."

"Meow."

She hopped out of the tub and did a panicked turn around the bathroom, dripping water everywhere. "I need to jam up your bells." She opened all the drawers and cabinets and rummaged through frantically. She stared at the curling iron and wondered whether she could melt the metal. "No." Tossing it aside, she held up a can of mousse. "Sticky, but not sticky enough." She tossed it aside. "There's got to be something."

"Meow."

Turning, she saw Thomas standing by the broken baseboard behind the toilet. On the floor was a caulk gun loaded with a tube of liquid nails from a repair she'd not finished. "Yes! Thomas, you're a genius!"

"Meow."

Picking up the caulk gun, she sat on the toilet and patted her knee. "Okay. Who wants to be first?"

Thomas jumped onto her lap. "Okay, baby. Stay still while I deal with this bell." Squinting, she carefully pushed a glob of liquid nails into the small hole in the bell's metal casing. Finished, she nodded. "Okay, Thomas. I'm going to kiss you. But you need to be careful. It takes fifteen minutes for the liquid nails to dry, and then several hours to cure."

"Meow."

She looked at him. His inky fur had the sheen of velvet. She better kiss him with him on her lap. If she crouched down to kiss him while he sat on the toilet, she would end up with her lips on his dick, just like she did with Johnny.

"Okay," she said. "Here goes nothing." She bent over but couldn't reach his nose. He stood on his hind legs, his front paws resting on her chest, and nosed her pursed lips.

Then she had a naked black man on her lap, his hands gripping her breasts.

"Thank you." He stood and stretched his broad, athletic frame. "You don't know how good it feels to stand upright." He cracked his back.

Wow was he beautiful. He was as carved as a Greek statue. Her mouth hung open.

Before she could say anything more, Harry jumped on her lap and meowed.

Chapter Five

"Eager for your turn, huh?" Niecy picked up the caulk gun and readied it while Harry settled on her lap. She scratched his chin absentmindedly. "Let me guess. You're an orange cat, so you're a red head."

He tapped her wrist twice with his paw.

"Oh, I guess I'm wrong." She snickered. "Well, I look forward to seeing what you look like." She really did. If he looked half as good as the other two, he'd still be a ten. And she enjoyed looking at man-chest; the covers on her smutty novels were one of her favorite parts.

Sitting naked on the toilet, she concentrated on filling his bell with the liquid nails. Once finished, she set the caulk gun on the floor. "Alright, Harry, you ready to be a man again?"

"Meow."

She picked him up under his arms and held him in front of her as she stood. "Let's try it this way. Cats always land on their feet, right?" She brought him to her lips and kissed his nose. That turned out to be the best way, because instantly he stood before her, no awkward dick licking or tit grabbing.

"Woohoo!" Harry grabbed Niecy's face between both hands and kissed her hard on the mouth. "God, I love you! You're the best!"

She blinked and stepped back, taking him in. "So not a red head. You're Asian."

"I'm Chinese."

Niecy chewed her lip as she drank him in. Woof. Harry was sexy as hell—another specimen of manliness fine enough to be a marble statue. She shifted her gaze to Thomas, and her hands itched to pet his abs. No one moved. She stared at them, and they stared at her.

She didn't feel the need to cover herself. These two had watched her bathe a least a hundred times. They watched her get off, too. Maybe they liked the way she looked, like Johnny, and unlike Preston. "Did you watch me play with my vibrator because you liked it?"

Thomas growled something resembling the word, "yes."

Harry flushed and looked at the floor. "Please don't be angry. You're just so beautiful when you come. Watching your pleasure was the highlight of my day."

She sucked in a sharp breath. Filthy thoughts invaded her mind. Sometimes she read smutty novels about a woman with two or more men. Here was her chance to try it. She'd bet they'd be willing, considering their voyeuristic pastimes. "Has it been a hundred years since either of you had sex, too?" she asked.

They both nodded. "We got cursed together with Johnny by the she-devil donkey," Thomas explained.

"A she-devil donkey?" This momentarily distracted Niecy from the double dicking down she now hoped to experience.

"Yes. She's—"

There was a knock on the bathroom door. "Niecy? Are you okay? I heard voices," Alyssa called from the other side. "Can I come in? I need to get Preston's cologne collection."

"Hold on a second," Niecy called back to Alyssa. "I'm just getting out of the bath." Locating her phone on the sink counter, she gave the two men an apologetic look. "I'm sorry," she whispered. "But I need you to be cats until I can get rid of her. There's no place for me to hide two naked men in here, and you can't lurk around outside like that."

Before they could protest, she pressed a ring tone sample in the settings menu on her phone. "I promise I'll turn you back as soon as I can. I want you to tell me about the donkey who cursed you. Just wait on the bathtub. She won't notice you." She reached into the water and pulled the plug to drain it. Then wrapped a towel around her body and used a clip to secure it above her breasts.

She opened the bathroom door. Alyssa stood there, her face puffy and red from crying. Niecy frowned. She never could stand seeing her baby sister cry.

"What's going on Lissy?"

Alyssa collapsed into Niecy's arms and sobbed. "I made a huge mistake," she wailed. "I don't know why I got caught up with him. He's—he's abusive and awful. He was never good enough for you, and I wanted you to break up with him for years. But then, I don't know, it's like he put me under a spell. Now I've done an awful thing to you, and you'll never forgive me, and you're my only family. I wish I could turn back time and change everything."

Steering her to sit on the bed, Niecy made soothing noises at Alyssa. "Take a breath, Lissy. Preston's a Douchasaurus Rex. But I can't really blame you for getting caught in his d-bag tractor beam when the exact same thing happened to me."

"I betrayed you in the worst way." She cried, then hiccupped. "Being with him is like mind-control. I honestly don't understand why I did this to you, and I feel terrible about it. It was like I couldn't stop. I couldn't say no to him."

Niecy walked to the closet and scooped up a pile of Preston's shoes, dropping them into a box. "Alyssa, you're only twenty-two. You're allowed to make some mistakes. I did. In fact, we both made the same mistake: dating Captain Douchecanoe." She dropped a pair of his Louboutins into the box with a sneer. "For the last year, ever since we started living together, I realized that my relationship with him was the symptom of a larger trauma. Studying social work has been useful because I'm better able to notice and name things, like automatic behavior patterns that come from trauma."

Alyssa rubbed her eyes. "Trauma? Like what? Our parents dying? You dated him for three years before they died."

Niecy picked up more of Preston's shoes and tossed them in the box. That man had more shoes than she did. "Our parents died because they drove off a cliff, Lissy."

"I know."

"Yeah. And you also know they drove off a cliff because they were drunk."

"Mm-hmm."

"Which was the least surprising thing ever, because they were always drunk. I mean, look at the disrepair of this house, of the entire property. This is how we grew up, in neglect and decay and chaos."

"Well, they were alcoholics. I'm just glad they didn't crash while we were in the car. How many times did they drive us around drunk when we were kids? Sometimes I think it's a miracle we're both alive."

"Exactly my point. Growing up with alcoholics fucked us up, Lissy. It screwed up our self-esteem and our sense of normalcy. It makes us question ourselves, our own experiences and judgment. A fuckface doucherocket like Preston takes advantage of damaged people, and that's what he did to both of us. He gaslit and broke us down, until I didn't know what was true about myself, and you didn't know what was right or wrong."

Niecy thought about having one of her cats piss into his shoes, but dismissed the idea, lest he get another court order. "Frankly, you did me a favor. I should've broken up with him years ago. I was just afraid I'd always be alone. But now I realize being alone with my cats and my books is a far better fate than staying with an abusive narcissist."

She sighed and looked at her little sister. "I'm not even heartbroken about him, but I am heartbroken about you." Niecy sat next to Alyssa on the edge of her bed, putting an arm around her shoulders. "You need to dump him, too. Get away from him. Make different mistakes with different men than the ones I made mistakes with."

Alyssa frowned. "Mistakes? Does that mean we're destined to date jackholes for the rest of our lives because we had terrible childhoods?"

Niecy laughed without humor. "Maybe, but I hope not. I hope I can make better choices. We both need to work on ourselves to get past our upbringing. You should go back to college and get away from the memories of mom and dad. You can't work at the coffee shop forever."

"I know." Tears leaked out of Alyssa's eyes again. "I'm so sorry for betraying you, Niecy. Will you ever forgive me?"

"Right now, I'm angry and hurt. I'm going to need some time. First, you need to break up with Preston. After that, we can repair our relationship. You'll need to show me I can trust you again, and that you're working on yourself, so this doesn't happen again."

Alyssa sniffed. "Okay. I'll do whatever it takes."

Niecy smiled at her sister. "You can start by getting the rest of Preston's shit out of here, so I never have to see him again." She located her phone where she'd tossed it on the bed and unblocked her sister's number while Alyssa finished gathering Preston's things from the bathroom.

Fifteen minutes later, most of Preston's personal effects had been tossed haphazardly into boxes and carried out to the living room. Niecy steered Alyssa out of her bedroom. "I love you, but I need some space. You can sit on the couch or on the front porch and neatly pack the boxes so he doesn't freak out on you. While you're at it, think about what you did and how you're going to make it up to me. Maybe free lattes every morning for, like, at least a month."

Alyssa giggled. "Okay. I'll see you tomorrow, newly single, latte in hand. I love you, too."

Abandoning Alyssa in the living room, Niecy hustled back to her bedroom and locked the door. Thomas and Harry sat on her bed. Despite the serious conversation she'd had with her sister, Niecy's mind never wandered far from her recently formed fantasy of a threesome. Being alone with her cats and smutty stories was, in fact, a massively positive turn in her life. That fact alone made it hard for her to stay mad at Alyssa.

Niecy pressed her back against the door. With a naughty gleam in her eye, she dropped her towel onto the floor. She smiled a sultry smile at Thomas and Harry. "As you interrupted my time in the bath with my vibrator, I expect you to make it up to me."

Chapter Six

N iecy walked up to the bed and kneeled before Harry, knowing full well where her mouth would end up. "You get to go first this time. Come here and kiss me." She closed her eyes and pursed her lips.

As soon as his dick tapped her chin, she opened wide and took him all the way to the back of her throat. She sucked hard as she pulled back, opening her eyes and looking up at him as she did. A groan rumbled from his throat, and he swallowed hard, making his Adam's apple rise and fall.

He pushed her hair off her forehead. "Holy shit, Niecy. I love you even more now, and I didn't think that was possible."

Smiling around his cock, she sucked Harry slowly for several more minutes until a paw smacked her cheek. Pulling off Harry, she rumbled a laugh. "I didn't forget about you, Thomas."

Shifting to crouch in front of Thomas, she pursed her lips. "Okay, your turn." A moment later, she had his cock in her mouth, and she savored sucking him slowly, looked up at him through her eyelashes.

After several minutes, she moved back to Harry's dick, bobbing her head faster and using her tongue, while pumping Thomas in her fist. Thomas was quieter than Harry, but he breathed a little harder when she twisted her wrist and pulsed her grip as she stroked.

Harry pressed the back of her head with his palm, pulling lightly on her hair, and moving her head faster. "Fuck, that feels good," he groaned.

Playing with their two cocks, she was so turned on that she felt her arousal slicking the inside of her thighs. Her pussy throbbed. Releasing both of them, she climbed onto the bed on all-fours. The quicker of the two, Harry was behind her immediately, digging his fingers into her hips while he dragged his tongue through her wet center. She jerked when his tongue flicked her clit.

Harry pulled back, replacing his tongue with his fingers, stroking circles around her clit while she quivered. "I memorized how you touched yourself, with your hand and your vibrator. I studied every move, so I would know how to please you if I ever got the chance."

She motioned for Thomas to kneel on the bed in front of her. Harry skillfully fingered her, bringing her to the edge of orgasm, but not letting her come. Niecy's moans of appreciation were muffled by Thomas's cock, which she sucked enthusiastically. Her eyes slid shut as her fantasy-come-true overwhelmed her.

"Do you want him to fuck you while you suck my cock?" Thomas asked, his hands in her hair.

"Mm-hmm."

"Look at me." Thomas pushed her firmly on the back of her head, making her take him until she gagged and her eyes watered. "Keep your eyes open." She obeyed, focusing her attention on him even as Harry thrust into her pussy.

The sensations enraptured her, and soon she was unable to concentrate on what she was doing with her mouth. She whimpered as Thomas took over, holding her head still and fucking her face with long, steady strokes. The sight of his cock gliding between her lips, over and over, while she was simultaneously being fucked from behind, thrilled her.

Harry's fingers dug into her waist as he fucked her slow. Her arms and legs burned as she braced to keep herself steady, pushing back to meet Harry's strokes. Harry pulled back, pausing with his tip at her entrance. Before she could protest, he slapped her ass with a sharp crack, and then pushed in roughly.

Her mouth went slack, despite being filled with Thomas's thick erection, and she cried out.

Harry hummed in satisfaction. "Oh, you liked that."

"Mm-hmm."

She pulled off Thomas's cock and lowered her head so she could suck on his balls and jerk him while angling her hips higher for Harry. After a few minutes, Thomas pulled out of her grasp. "I'm going to come in your hair if you keep that up."

Leaving Thomas alone for a moment, she lowered her front half until her forehead rested on the mattress. She rolled her hips and took Harry's cock, pushing against his thrusts. He got a little rougher, spanking her as he fucked her until she shook uncontrollably. "Oh, yes, fuck me!" An orgasm rolled through her.

"That's it, Niecy. Come for me." Harry panted, not letting up.

When her orgasm receded, he pulled out. She collapsed onto the mattress, her limbs like jelly.

"Did we wear you out already?" Thomas asked, slowly stroking his cock as he kneeled above her.

She sat up, a sly grin spreading across her face. "No way. In fact, I'd like to try something. Get on your back." She scooted over until he stretched out on the bed next to her. "I want to ride your cock, Thomas." She straddled him, lining him up and sliding down his dick. Her pussy clenched around him, and she moaned.

Once she had him comfortably inside her, she folded forward, pressing her breasts to Thomas's chest. She took a deep breath and voiced her desire while moving up and down his cock. "I want Harry to fuck my ass. I want to feel you both inside me. I want you to fill me up with your cocks and with your cum."

Thomas responded by cupping her cheeks and kissing her until she was panting and riding him faster. She didn't stop riding Thomas while Harry found the lube in the nightstand.

When he returned to the bed, Harry soaked her ass with the lube, and then primed her with his finger. She moaned from pleasure as his stroking finger stimulated all her nerves and widened her asshole to take his cock. When he pulled his finger out, she stilled so that he could enter her.

Taking a deep breath and relaxing, she enjoyed the novel sensation of him mounting her from behind, sliding fully into her while Thomas's dick filled her pussy. It felt amazing. The pressure on all her nerve endings from their two dicks made her vibrate.

She'd tried anal before but hadn't enjoyed it because Preston was selfish and rough, and she was never adequately lubricated. She loved it now. Quickly finding their rhythm, they all moved in unison, making her and the mattress's springs scream. Her sister might overhear, but she didn't care. It felt too good for her to be quiet.

When Thomas and Harry increased the speed and depth of their thrusts, wave after wave of ecstasy crashed over her. She jerked with one orgasm after another, loudly encouraging them to fuck her like animals. Their grunts and groans filled her ears. She wasn't sure who came first, but soon they were both pulsing and jerking inside her, sending her over the edge again. Then they all collapsed in a sweaty, panting mess of tangled bodies.

After a moment, Harry pulled out and went to the bathroom for toilet paper. Niecy rolled off Thomas and onto her back. "That was amazing. I've never experienced anything like it."

He got up. "Not bad for a couple of guys who haven't had sex in a century."

She laughed. "Not bad at all."

Climbing out of her bed, he headed toward the bathroom. "Want to do it again in the shower?"

She vaguely worried about making herself sore from all the dick she'd been getting, but decided she didn't care. "Oh yeah."

As she carefully stood on wobbly legs, she saw a missed text on her phone.

Alyssa:

Are you having sex?

Niecy:

Yup

Alyssa:

Who? How? I didn't see anyone come in

Niecy:

They came in through the window

Alyssa:
They???

Niecy:
Two extremely hot guys

Alyssa:
At the same time???

Niecy:
10/10, would recommend

Alyssa:
What??? I'm gonna need details

Niecy:
Some other time. They're waiting for me in the shower

Alyssa:
You're my hero. Get it, girl

Niecy:
I was starved after five years of Douche McGouche's pencil dick

Alyssa:
lol

Douche McGouche. It reminded her of Johnny. She needed to go find him at the crumbling one-room church at the edge of her property.

She listened to the water running in the bathroom. She should shower first, as she was a sweaty, sticky mess. And if she got tag-teamed again, well, that's just how things went. Just a quickie, though. That's all she had time for.

Two hours later, Niecy returned home from the Walmart with a bag of men's clothes: boxers, T-shirts, sweats, and three pairs of slides for their feet. She'd have to get them something more suitable later, when she could bring them to the store and be sure of the fit. Alyssa and Preston's things were gone from her porch.

She set the bags of clothes on the living room coffee table. Thomas and Harry sat on towels on her sofa, scarfing Doritos. She smiled. "As much as I enjoy looking at you two in the buff, I need you to get dressed." She handed Thomas a roll of paper towels from off the table. "You're covered in cheese dust."

"I've never tasted anything like these," Thomas said. "They're amazing. I've really missed food."

"I promise I'll make you the best dinner when we get back. I bought steaks, macaroni and cheese, beer, and cookie dough ice cream."

"You did?" Harry jumped off the sofa and wrapped her in a bear hug, getting cheese dust on her shirt. "You're the greatest woman on the planet!"

She blushed, pushing back from him. "C'mon, we got to go. Now that Alyssa and Sir Doucherton are gone, we need to get

Johnny. While we're walking, you can tell me about the donkey who cursed you."

While they dressed, she packed a backpack with clothes for Johnny, some food and water, a first-aid kit (just in case), and the caulk gun loaded with liquid nails. Thomas insisted on carrying it for her as they began the half-mile track through the trees to the decaying church.

It'd been years since she'd been there. She hadn't ventured out to it since she inherited the house. Last time she saw the crumbling structure, it had been little more than four walls, a few rotting pews and pulpit, broken windows, and no roof.

She used to play there with Alyssa when they were kids. They would play hide-and-go-seek and hold pretend weddings until she got older and realized the unstable structure was dangerous. Then she told Alyssa they weren't allowed to play there anymore. She'd been Alyssa's substitute parent since she was eight. She wondered how much of their childhood Johnny, Harry, and Thomas had observed.

Lost in thought, she stumbled over a rock hidden in the grass. With cat-like reflexes, Harry grabbed her by the arm and steadied her. He kept a protective hand on her lower back as they continued through the trees.

She glanced at him. "So, about that donkey ... I'd like the whole story, please."

"As you wish." He took a deep breath. "I worked with Johnny and Thomas in the old copper mine. The one that's closed now after it flooded. For years, we worked in the dark, blowing open new passages with dynamite and finding copper veins. Every few years, we would get a new donkey who would haul the rubble and ore out of the mine for us. That was cheaper than motors back then. The donkeys would work with us until they went blind, and then we'd get a new one."

"I'd been working in the mines since I was a boy, about twelve," Thomas chimed in. "Same with Johnny. Since we were around the same age, we rented a room together, worked on the same crew together, and did everything together. Harry joined our crew in his early twenties after getting in some trouble at home."

"I got caught kissing a prominent politician's daughter and had to flee," Harry explained with a laugh. "They were white."

Niecy frowned, glad she didn't have to experience life as a woman from a hundred years before. "Things must've been really different back then."

"They were," Thomas said. "We've only been able to observe how things have changed over the last century by watching people and then watching TV. I wonder how much we truly understood, as observers and not participants. I'm curious how we'll get along, if we're ever able to lift this blasted curse."

"You will. I'll make sure of it." Niecy petted his forearm. "So how did you get cursed? If I'm going to break it, I must know how it started."

Chapter Seven

Harry's jaw muscles worked before he continued the story. "One day, the donkey we were working with bolted. She ran out of the mine and through the forest until she got to the church. It was the mining town's only chapel back then, and most folk went to it on Sundays." His eyes looked off into the distance, watching his memories. "Mine-trained donkeys were worth a lot back then—more than men, I reckon. We would've lost wages for the better part of the year if we didn't catch her. So we chased her all the way to the church."

"As soon as she stepped onto the holy ground, she turned into a beautiful, naked woman," Thomas said.

"Just like you guys?" Niecy asked.

Thomas nodded. "Exactly."

"In fact, she was luring us," Harry added. "She wanted us to follow her. We were shocked when she turned into a woman. Johnny handed her his coat to cover her nudity and asked her where she came from. He's the most chivalrous of us three."

Thomas chuckled. "And you've always been the one who got into trouble chasing the ladies. But that day, chasing after her, all three of us found trouble."

"She told us she was cursed," Harry said, continuing the story. "She said the curse had no power on consecrated land and inside holy places, but she would return to being a donkey as soon as she stepped off the church's grounds. She asked us to free her from the curse."

Thomas's expression turned grim as he took over the storytelling. "She led us to a book hidden behind a false wall in the lectern on the pulpit. It was a book of ancient curses, and she turned to a page and pointed at one. We can all read now, but back then, I was the only one of us who could. She asked me to read the text out loud, but it couldn't be done at the church because the magic didn't work there, even to break the enchantment that tortured her."

Harry's hand moved from Niecy's lower back to her hip, and he pulled her into his side, as though her presence was his ward against evil. "She said we all needed to touch her while Thomas read the spell, and that would return her to human form. Then she walked out of the church, and we all talked about it. We knew that if we didn't return with a donkey, we'd be indentured to the mine for a year. But we decided freeing her was the right thing to do, anyway, so we agreed."

"No good deed goes unpunished," Thomas said. "We did free her. But the curse wasn't broken; it was transferred. She turned us into cats. She called us her little pusses. Said she'd fallen in love with us after years together in the mines, and she wanted to keep us to be her lovers. Then she stuck these blasted collars on our necks." Thomas snorted angrily. "My parents were slaves, and even though I worked in a mine, I was proud I was free. In an instant, that evil bitch enslaved us and took the only thing we had: our freedom."

Niecy whimpered, her heart breaking for her three men. "That's so awful."

Harry glanced down at Niecy, whom he still pressed into his side. "After she turned us into cats, she took us to an abandoned cottage that stood where your house is now. When we got there, she modified the curse. She made it so we would return to human form when we were kissed by someone who loved us. But we'd return to cat form at the ring of a bell. She planned to turn us into men to serve her at her whim, and then she would ring a bell when she was done with us, that way we wouldn't leave."

Thomas chuckled mirthlessly. "The joke was on her, though. What she did was too selfish to be called love. So it didn't matter how much she kissed us, we stayed cats."

Harry dug a finger under his collar and snapped it against his skin. "In a fit of frustration, she fitted us with these belled collars and enchanted them so that we couldn't take them off. She made it so they can't come off until the curse gets lifted. And that would never happen. We would never be men again, because who would love a bunch of abandoned, stray cats?"

"I would," Niecy said, fury filling her chest. "Bitch! If she's still alive,—I don't know how being a she-devil donkey-lady works—I'm going to wring her neck with my bare hands."

"You don't need to," Harry said. "She was worth far more as a donkey than a woman. She was penniless, so she worked at the town brothel and died of syphilis a few years later."

"A tragic end," Niecy said, blowing out a breath. A deep sadness for her men, and for a woman who was twice cursed, made her body feel heavy.

"No one loved us for a century," Thomas said, pulling Niecy's attention back. He nudged her until she stepped away from Harry's side and stopped walking. Standing in front of her, Thomas took both of her hands and brought her knuckles to his lips. "Until you. I know this is sudden, and probably overwhelming for you, but it's not for us. We've loved you for a long time. You're the opposite of that she-devil donkey. You're everything beautiful and kind and perfect embodied in a single woman. I want to spend the rest of my life proving you were worth waiting a hundred years for."

Harry moved in closer and stroked her cheek. "Same goes for me. You have my heart and my devotion. I expect Johnny will tell you the same thing, too."

Niecy's mouth twisted, and tears sprung to her eyes. "Aww, you guys ..."

Harry chucked her on the chin. "C'mon now, sweetheart. No tears. Let's get Johnny and rid ourselves of this curse. The spell book is in the lectern. The donkey-witch left it in the cottage when she went to live at the brothel, so we returned it to the church for safekeeping. It took us three days to drag it half a mile as cats."

"About time you guys got here."

Niecy jumped at Johnny's voice. She'd been so engrossed in the story, she hadn't realized they'd arrived at the church. He sat a few feet away in the overgrown grass on a weathered grave-marker. "Johnny!" Niecy sprinted to him, dropping into his lap and peppering his face with kisses.

"Thank you for listening to me and running here. I'm sorry it took so long. It took hours, but I finally got rid of McGouche and all his crap, and I've made up with my sister, and I found out that Harry and Thomas were also cursed, and I put liquid nails in their bells so they can stay men, and I bought you all clothes," she babbled.

He shut her up with a kiss until she relaxed and curled contentedly against his chest. Pulling his lips from hers, he said, "You've been busy, my darling. I guess I can forgive you for making me wait all day."

"And we still have much to do." She climbed off Johnny's lap and stood. "Thomas, hand me the backpack so I can fix his bell." She gave a critical eye to Johnny's naked ass defiling some long-forgotten person's grave. "Also, you should put on pants."

After he dressed, Johnny wrapped his arms around Niecy and pressed her to his chest while she filled his bell with liquid nails. It took a little longer than it should because he wouldn't stop groping her and making her giggle.

Finally, she accomplished it. "Done." She dropped the caulk gun into her backpack and stepped back. "Alright, let's go find that book of curses." She tugged on Johnny's hand. "Show me where it's at."

A few minutes later, Johnny handed her the spell book from inside the rotting lectern. Niecy set it on the altar. The marble altar was in good shape, despite the church rotting around it, and resembled a simple table. As her feet were getting tired, she hopped onto the marble slab and leafed through the book. It was filled with nonsense poetry, like it was written by an emo teenager from the Middle Ages.

Johnny took the book from her hands and set it aside. "Now that you've stopped our bells from ringing, we have time to break the curse. I've got something else I'd rather do right now."

Niecy arched an eyebrow. "What's that?"

He hopped up onto the marble next to her and pulled her onto his lap. His mouth descended onto hers, and soon she was whimpering as he stole her breath and groped his hands up her shirt and under her bra.

A third hand, and then a fourth, slid under the hems of her shorts. The other two wanted to join. Her brain whited out from excitement.

Crawling off Johnny, she stood on the altar. Scanning her three men with her heated gaze, she slowly stripped out of her clothes, dropping each piece on the marble. The way they stared at her made her feel like the most beautiful woman in the world.

"You're a goddess," Johnny growled, still sitting at her feet.

"Oh, yeah?" One side of her lips tipped in a half-smile. "Worship me."

Harry sucked in a breath, whipped his clothes off, and was on the altar with his head between her legs before the other two stepped out of their pants. Harry put her thigh over his shoulder and devoured her pussy like it was dusted with Doritos flavoring.

She let out a throaty moan and threw her head back. "Someone better hold me up. My leg's going to give out."

In an instant, Thomas was behind her, supporting her weight and kissing her senseless.

Johnny joined them, pinching and twisting her nipples. He sucked a breast into his mouth when she arched back so far she was no longer standing. Her beautiful men supported her weight while they worshipped every inch of her body. She felt like she was levitating.

Carefully, they lowered her until her back was on the cool marble. Shifting so that both of her legs were over his shoulders, Harry used a finger to massage her g-spot as he tortured her clit with the flat of his tongue. Johnny and Thomas kneeled over her, their cocks engorged and in their fists.

Seeing how hard they were for her was the sexiest thing she'd ever experienced. She wanted them. She wanted all three of them at the same time. She rolled over and climbed onto her knees. "Johnny, get under me." As she moved to straddle him, she reached her hand into her pussy and rubbed her arousal back toward her ass. "Thomas, get behind me."

She alternated between Johnny's cock and Thomas's fingers so that Thomas could smear her wetness around. Then she filled her pussy with Johnny and swiveled her hips to grind her clit against him. His hands gripped her ass and spread her wide. Thomas filled her, pushing into her ass with a gentle deliberateness. "Oh, God," she groaned. "Both of you fucking me at once is my new favorite feeling. Please never stop fucking me."

"Happy to oblige, my darling," Johnny said between groans.

She quivered as they increased their pace. But she had one more hole to fill, and one more dick to please. She arched her back, raising her head. "Harry, I want you to fuck my mouth. Fuck me until you come down my throat. I want all three of you to fill me with your cum."

She didn't know where this newly confident sex-vixen had come from, but it felt great. Maybe it was because three of the hottest men she'd seen in her life loved her and wanted to ring her bell nonstop.

"Holy shit, you're hot," Harry said, as though he could read her mind. He guided her mouth onto his dick, pushing until she gagged and murmured her approval.

She braced as she took all three of her men, giving them full control over her body. Johnny's hands moved from her ass to her breasts, which he squeezed and massaged, brushing his thumbs over her sensitive nipples. Harry pulled her hair, making her scalp tingle. And Thomas gripped her hips, holding her up and keeping her steady.

Without warning, her orgasm ripped through her pelvis and up her spine. It felt so good she wanted to scream. But her cries were muffled by Harry's cum, which he poured down her throat with a shout. She swallowed it down, hot and thick, concentrating on breathing through her nose. He pulled out, and she licked a few remaining drops off his tip while he twitched.

She'd barely swallowed the last of Harry's cum when she felt Thomas increase his pace, pounding her ass so hard that his balls slapped her skin. She leaned down onto Johnny's chest, tilting her hips to give Thomas better access, while improving the friction of Johnny's cock against her clit. With the increased sensation, she came again, her pussy pulsing and tightening around Johnny, and her ass squeezing Thomas at the base.

Her orgasm set them both off. Thomas slammed into her twice more before he stilled and pumped his cum into her ass. Johnny sped up as he came, and the pressure on her clit made her vibrate like a live wire. Tears sprung into her eyes, and then she orgasmed once more.

They stopped moving before she did, letting Niecy experience her orgasm fully. She collapsed on top of Johnny after Thomas pulled out and took a deep, shuddering breath. "Wow, that was intense. Now I need a nap." She listened to their laughter and smiled, stretching like a kitten on top of Johnny's chest. Exhausted, she drifted, nearly falling to sleep.

"Niecy," Johnny rumbled softly beneath her. "Wake up, my darling. We should head back to the house."

"Yeah." She yawned. Reluctantly rolling off him, she dug into the first-aid kit and found some gauze to use as a tissue. After they tidied and dressed, she put the book of curses into her backpack and headed toward the yard. "Come on boys. I want to cook you dinner."

Chapter Eight

N iecy and her three men stayed loved up in her cottage for days, and it brought her immense joy to reacquaint them with the pleasures of being human. The only source of contention within the group had to do with sleeping arrangements. Her bed was not big enough, so the men rotated between sleeping with her and in the old bunk beds in the room she and Alyssa shared as children.

Making matters worse, Niecy avoided her childhood room altogether because Alyssa never showed up with lattes or to announce she'd dumped the doucheroo. Alyssa also ignored Niecy's texts but left the read-receipts on. Agitated by Alyssa breaking her promises, Niecy seethed and grieved. Letting her sister go felt like a death.

And then there was the curse. According to the book, the curse could not be broken. It could only be passed from victim to victim and had endured like a virus for centuries. The group argued about whether, and who, to pass the curse on to.

"We could find a murderer in prison," Harry suggested at as they sat for dinner three nights later.

Niecy shook her head. "If we could even get close enough to an unrepentant murderer to touch him and read the curse, the guards will surely notice that their prisoner has disappeared." The men grumbled their agreement.

"What about passing it on to one of the abusive people you come across as a social worker?" Thomas asked. "Someone who beats their spouse or children surely deserves it."

Niecy shook her head again. "No. It's unfair to deny someone a chance at redemption. The people I encounter all suffer from generational abuse and poverty. They can be rehabilitated if their trauma and difficulties are addressed. Cursing someone who has lived through abuse themselves is not the right way to break the cycle."

"You're so soft and loving," Thomas said. "You see the good, even in the worst people."

"You're too nice to me." Her lower lipped quivered. "Anyway, my parents were alcoholics. They weren't good parents, but they weren't evil. They were damaged, emotionally and physically, and never healed from it. It has taught me compassion for broken people."

Thomas leaned over the table and kissed her forehead.

"I've got it," Johnny exclaimed. "About thirty years ago, there was a little boy who lived nearby. He would catch and torture cats. I'm pretty sure he's still your neighbor and has moved onto bigger prey."

"Do you have proof of any of that?" Niecy asked.

"No."

"Then we can't curse him. He could be a nice person now. We don't know."

Johnny snorted. "Doubtful. Kids who torture cats rarely turn out to be normal adults."

"Do you have any ideas?" Harry asked Niecy, spearing a black olive off her plate. "Also, what's for dinner?"

She stood to unbox the takeout she'd picked up. "I don't think we should pass a cursed torch to other people. It's wrong. I'd rather we look for ways to break the curse instead. There must be something. Let's look for a few days before we discuss this anymore." The men groaned, but relented when she kissed them all on the head and introduced them to street tacos with carnitas and guacamole.

The next day, she scoured the internet and the archives at the local library. She called a priest. She even consulted a phone psychic. But the answer to breaking the curse remained elusive. In the meantime, she could turn them back to humans with her kisses if ever they heard a bell ring—which they did, several times.

From the TV to the microwave to the car to the sliding doors of the store, bells rang everywhere. She bought them noise-canceling headphones, which she paired to her phone and a bell-free playlist, just so they could leave the house.

After four days of being wrapped in the arms of her three lovers, she returned to work before she became bowlegged. Plus, frankly, she worried about the cost of feeding three hulking men. She needed to get her license and a pay raise as soon as possible.

When she got home that evening, the men had made several repairs to the house without being asked. They handed her a glass of wine and told her about the vegetable garden they were planting to help with the cost of food. Then they made dinner and washed the dishes, also without being asked, before ravishing her for an hour.

She wondered whether she'd died and gone to heaven.

That night, she slept tucked in the protective circle of Thomas's body. But when she woke in the early morning hours, worrying about the curse and her sister, she knew she wasn't in heaven just yet.

The following Saturday, as she didn't have to work, she brought them to the local coffee shop to introduce them to latte foam art. It was also a chance for her to confront Alyssa, whom she expected to be working the register.

The line was long. Eventually, Niecy reached the counter. "Four honey-vanilla lattes, please."

Alyssa startled and stared at the three fit men surrounding Niecy like bodyguards, her mouth agape. "Um, what names should I put on all the cups?"

"Niecy will be fine."

"You're not going to introduce me?"

"Nope."

Alyssa looked the men up and down. "Why are they wearing headphones?"

"To protect their ears from bells."

"What?" Alyssa frowned. "What aren't you telling me?" She lowered her voice to a whisper, leaning forward. "Are these the men you were having sex with the other day? I thought it was two."

"It's three now." Niecy shrugged, trying to keep her seething anger bottled up.

"At once?" Alyssa gasped in a loud, shocked voice.

"Lower your voice," Niecy hissed. "Anyway, it's none of your business. I don't even know you anymore. You broke our relationship."

Biting her lip, Alyssa looked down at the register and pressed some buttons. "That'll be $22.13."

Niecy crossed her arms. "That'll be zero for me. You owe me an entire week of lattes. Would it be easier if I just ran a tab? Maybe I should get some cinnamon rolls, too. My boys love to eat. They burn a lot of calories at night."

Alyssa's cheeks pinked. "Okay. Yeah. I'll get it. And four cinnamon rolls. Go find a table and I'll bring your order out."

A few minutes later, Alyssa served their coffees and cinnamon rolls. Niecy watched her setting down the plates and suddenly realized how thin her sister looked. When Alyssa bent over, the neckline of her blouse gapped and revealed a bony shoulder ... and a bunch of bruises on her neck.

Niecy launched to her feet, startling the men, who also jumped up. She pinched Alyssa's chin and turned her face. "Why are you wearing so much foundation? You never wear makeup."

Alyssa looked away. "Preston likes me made up."

"Is that so?" She tugged on Alyssa's neckline to get a better view of the bruises. "Where did you get these bruises from? Did Preston do that to you? Tell me, Lissy."

Alyssa looked at Niecy, her eyes brimming with tears. "Please don't tell anyone," she whispered. "When I tried to break up with him, he got so upset he choked me. Afterward, he apologized and begged my forgiveness. When I refused, he said I didn't have a choice. He said no one would believe me over him. He blamed you for putting ideas in my head, and I'm not allowed to talk to you. He checks my phone. He'll hurt you if he finds out I told you."

Alyssa shook like a leaf, so Niecy pulled her into a close hug to steady her. "Let me help you, Lissy. You can stay with me."

Alyssa jerked. "No. It won't work. His parents will make sure I can't get a restraining order, and he'd never be charged if he hurt us. He could murder us on the street in front of everyone, and he'd still get away with it."

Niecy gestured toward her three companions. "He won't bother us. I've got protection. He's just one douche. He's no match against five of us."

Alyssa took a shuddering breath. "What about when I want to go out. I can't stay inside your house forever."

"Don't worry. It'll be temporary. He'll lose interest before self-reflection can kick in. Come home; I'll keep you safe, Lissy, like I always have."

Alyssa nodded. "Okay. I'll tell my boss I'm sick and leave with you guys. Finish your lattes first. Preston's not expecting me for another two hours."

An hour later, they walked through the front door of Niecy's house, and the men took their headphones off. "What's going on?" Johnny asked immediately.

"Preston hurt Alyssa. She has to stay here with us for her safety."

Alyssa stuck out her hand. "Hi, guys. Nice to meet you. What are your names?"

Niecy pointed to each man, introducing them. "This is Johnny, Thomas, and Harry."

"Like your cats?" Alyssa cocked her head.

"Exactly." Niecy snickered.

Alyssa looked around. "Wow, the house looks fantastic. Better than when we first moved here as kids. You've been busy."

"The boys have been fixing things while I'm at work." Niecy smiled broadly. "They're the best."

"I'm not jealous at all." Alyssa gave her a goofy smile. "Can I make everyone lunch?"

They'd just finished eating when Preston showed up. He pounded on the door and screamed. "Alyssa! I know you're in there! Get out here right now!"

Niecy ran up to the door, shouting through it. "Fuck off, Preston! You're not welcome here. Alyssa doesn't want to see you anymore. You need to leave her alone."

"Shut up, Niecy, you stupid, fat cow. No one cares what you think. Don't ruin your sister's future by turning her into a pathetic cat lady like you." He pounded on the door again.

Niecy jerked at his insults. "Go eat a bag of dicks!"

"If I did, that'll be more dick than you'll get in a lifetime. No one wants you, and you're just jealous that you couldn't keep me, when Alyssa could. Go back to your smut and cookie dough."

Alyssa ran to the door, her voice tremulous. "Stop it, Preston. Don't talk to her like that. Please just go away."

There was a thump on the door as Preston leaned against it and lowered his voice to an almost soothing level. "Come on, bunny. Come out. I just want to talk. I promise I won't get mad. I love you. Your sister's confusing you and trying to ruin your life. Don't let her."

Niecy snorted. "I told you to leave, Preston. You're trespassing. Leave before I call the cops."

He laughed. "Call the cops on *me*? You really are a stupid cunt."

Harry appeared next to Niecy and eased her and Alyssa back until they stood behind him. Then, in one swift movement, he opened the door and had Preston by the collar, lifting him onto his toes. "You will never disrespect Niecy again, do you understand?"

"Who the fuck are you?" Preston asked in a strangled voice.

Harry ignored his question. "Not only will you never disrespect her again, you'll never talk to her again. You are not worthy of being in her presence. Now scram."

Preston held his hands up in surrender. "Okay. Okay. I'm leaving." When Harry set him back on his feet, Preston stretched his neck and fixed his collar. "Come on, bunny. Let's go."

"She's not going anywhere," Niecy snapped.

"She's my girlfriend, and it's time for her to come home," Preston countered, his normally smooth voice cracking.

"Were you not listening?" Harry said. "The lady says she doesn't want to see you anymore."

"Stop interfering," Preston snarled. "You can have Niecy to satisfy your slumming fetish, or whatever, but my relationship with Alyssa is none of your concern."

Lightning quick, Harry decked Preston so hard he stumbled backward off the porch and landed on the grass. "I told you, you will not disrespect Niecy," Harry growled. "Do you not understand English?"

Preston got up and cracked his knuckles. "That was a sucker punch. Come fight me like a man, pussy." He rushed up the steps but skidded to a halt when Thomas and Johnny appeared on the porch next to Harry. "Can't fight me fair, so you need to call your pussy friends, I see," Preston sneered, nevertheless backing up a few steps.

Thomas crossed his arms. "Leave, and don't come back. We will always be here, and we've fought tougher men than you."

"Naw," Johnny drawled, glancing at Thomas. "I'm good with him continuing to piss us off. Nothing would please me more than breaking his nose."

"That could be fun," Harry agreed.

In the far distance, church bells rang. As it was a Saturday afternoon, someone must've gotten married.

And then the men were cats struggling to climb out of a pile of clothes.

Niecy slapped her hands over her mouth in horror.

Alyssa screamed.

Preston gasped. "What the fuck kind of witchcraft is this?" He kneeled to inspect the cats and the clothes. "These are your stray cats. You turned your cats into men, Niecy? How the fuck ...? Is this what you've been doing at night, while you neglected me? Were you in the woods fucking your cats, like some Satanic pervert?"

Not knowing how to explain, Niecy stammered. "They were my cats, but not anymore ... You can't hurt them because they're men ..."

Preston retched. "I can't believe you turned your cats into men, rather than work on improving your value to real men. That's fucking disgusting, Niecy. Unnatural. You're pathetic."

With a savage yowl, Johnny ran up Preston's pant leg. He swiped viciously at Preston's face with his claws. Preston grabbed Johnny by the scruff and peeled him off, holding him at arm's length as Johnny twisted and hissed.

Preston stomped up the steps and into the living room, kicking Harry and Thomas across the porch as he passed.

"Alyssa, we're leaving. Time to go." Preston clutched Johnny by the throat.

Alyssa stood rooted in place, her face white as a sheet.

"I said, move it," Preston snarled.

She shook her head and mouthed the word, "no."

"Get into the car, or I will snap the neck of your sister's precious cat, followed by every other cat here, until you move your ass." He squeezed Johnny's throat until Johnny's mouth hung open and his tongue lolled.

"No! Don't hurt him," Alyssa whispered.

"Don't hurt him?" Preston lifted his chin and looked down his nose at Alyssa. "Beg, bunny."

Alyssa slowly lowered to her knees. "Please, my king. I'll be good. I'm sorry. You're right. I got confused. I'm better now. Please, just put him down and let's go. I'll never question you again."

While Preston focused on Alyssa, his lip curled into a self-satisfied sneer, Niecy crept to the coffee table and opened the spell book. Her voice trembling, she read aloud:

> *My heart is battered, black and blue.*
> *I cannot live life without you.*
> *Forsooth, you are my one true love.*
> *We fit together, hand-in-glove.*
> *You forsook me and now must pay,*
> *As an animal, live each day.*
> *Pain's eternal, outliving death.*
> *This curse endures long past my breath.*

The house shook, causing Niecy to drop the book. Then, where Preston had stood a moment before, sat a floppy-eared rabbit ... and Johnny in man form.

Johnny rose and reached for the clasp on his collar. It popped off. "Niecy. You broke the curse."

"No, I didn't break it. I transferred it to Preston. Now he's a rabbit." Her mouth twisted. "He's a terrible person, but I didn't want to pass the curse along. We can put him in a hutch for safekeeping, and I'll keep looking for a cure."

Upon hearing this, Preston hopped around in a frantic circle. Alyssa crawled over and picked him up, cradling him to her breast. "Calm down, you stupid bunny. You'll give yourself a heart attack. If anyone can figure out how to break a curse, it'll be Niecy, so you best be a nice bunny."

Thomas and Harry appeared in the doorway. They had their pants on and their collars off. Thomas threw a pair of jeans at Johnny. "Cover your junk. There are ladies present."

The chapel bells rang again. Niecy held her breath, but her men stayed men. Relieved, she sprinted to Thomas and Harry and gave them both kisses. Then she ran to Johnny and checked his throat for marks. "I told you not to do that! You scared me half to death!"

"I'll never do that again."

"Good!"

Smirking, he added, "because I'll never be a cat again. As a man, I'll knock out any asshole who threatens you."

She huffed and gave him a light shove on the shoulder.

"What?" He cupped her face and kissed her.

Niecy pressed into Johnny's side and turned to face Thomas and Harry. "Get dressed, boys. Now that you can no longer be turned into cats at the ring of a bell, I'm taking you to the casino. They have an amazing seafood buffet with crab legs and fish tacos."

"Fish tacos?" Harry asked.

Niecy grinned. "Trust me, you'll love them."

More from Amelia Elliot

Looking for more saucy sophisticated stories? Check out Amelia Elliot's *Thunderstruck* Series.

https://linktr.ee/ameliaelliot

    Amelia Elliot writes smart romance for discerning readers. When she's not writing fiction, Ms. Elliot works as a trial lawyer, copywriter, and non-fiction author on topics of law, business, and politics. As someone with chronic illness, Ms. Elliot writes stories about hope overcoming trauma and adversity from an "own voices" viewpoint. She lives with her husband and their three big dogs.

www.ingramcontent.com/pod-product-compliance
Lightning Source LLC
Chambersburg PA
CBHW030939260626
47169CB00002B/536